DESPERATE

BY

SYLVIA MCDANIEL

SYLVIA McDANIEL

DESPERATE

A LIPSTICK AND LEAD NOVEL

They always get their man.

Cover by Lyndsey Lewellen

Chapter One

1876

"**I** don't believe you. My sister was not charging boys to kiss her," Meg McKenzie said, standing in the field of her small East Texas family farm in her father's hand-me-downs.

Her sister's schoolteacher stood in front of Meg with her arms folded, her expression filled with contempt, her nose wrinkling up in disdain.

This was her fourth trip out to the farm this year. Surely by now, the schoolmarm had grown accustomed to the smell of manure that permeated Meg's clothing. Certainly, she knew Meg worked the farm alone, which was not for the faint of heart, and most definitely, she had to know Meg could barely tolerate the woman who wasn't much older than herself.

Meg closed her eyes and wished for the thousandth time she lived the life of a normal young girl. With a living mother and a father who spent time at home. That she had a life of dancing, pretty dresses, and young men courting.

When she reopened her eyes, Meg recognized the poke bonnet and a bustle beneath the teacher's skirt from the last catalogue Papa had brought home. The woman

1

was wearing the latest fashion. Fashions Meg longed to design. Fashions Meg wanted to wear. Fashions that would make Meg feel like a woman, rather than an ugly hoyden.

"She was kissing boys," the woman repeated. The schoolmarm's reddening cheeks and narrowed eyes bespoke of the temper she seemed barely restraining as she confronted Meg about Ruby's bad behavior.

At nineteen, Meg felt too young to be the responsible parent of a fifteen-year-old. And her sister, Ruby was definitely more than one person could handle.

"I'm sorry, Meg. I know you've had to raise this child without much help from your father, but I can't have her coming back to school. She's a distraction in the classroom," the refined woman told Meg, her parasol shielding her from the hot midday sun.

For a moment, Meg wanted to reach out her hand to touch the silky fabric of the woman's dress. But knew that would be wrong. Yet she longed to know what such rich material felt like.

They stood in the pasture where Meg had been hoeing as she prepared the spring garden for planting. Mud coated her work pants, she smelled of animals and sweat, and her hands were calloused and rough from time spent working the land. This was not the life she wanted for herself. Meg dreamed of being a woman who had few responsibilities and wasn't accountable for the care of the farm and her two sisters. She didn't want to be a parent.

And Ruby seemed to stay in trouble. "My sister may not have had a mother to raise her properly, but she's been taught that girls don't chase boys."

"She wasn't chasing them, Meg. She was charging

them a nickel a piece to kiss her," Miss Andrews said, her parasol held tightly in her gloved hands.

Meg couldn't help herself; she laughed. Not even Ruby would be foolish enough to do something so naughty. "I don't believe you."

Miss Andrews placed her hand on her hip and almost snarled at Meg. "I would never have found out about it, if the line hadn't gone clear around the building. I caught her in the act of kissing Jimmy Brown."

"Oh," Meg said, her brows drawing down into a scowl. Could Ruby have been so stupid? At first, Meg couldn't believe what the teacher was telling her, but when she thought about it, Ruby was at a stage in her life when she seemed intrigued with boys. "I'm sure she has a perfectly good explanation for her behavior. I'll talk to her."

The teacher took a step towards Meg, a frown on her scholarly face. "I'm sorry, but that's not good enough. She would have graduated next month anyway. Let's just say she'll receive her certificate showing she completed school in the tenth grade. I don't think I can teach her anything else." The woman lowered her voice, muttering under her breath, "She might be able to teach me some things."

"She's a kid. A girl who's curious," Meg said, defending her sister. Yes, Ruby was troublesome, but she was not a bad girl, just someone perplexed about the changes going on in her young woman's body. Ruby was highly intelligent, easily bored, and often mischievous if left to her own devices.

The schoolmarm raised her brows in an insolent way. "Well, she's training the students in a subject that neither boys nor the girls in my classroom need to learn at this time in their life."

A rush of fury tightened Meg's chest at the contempt she sensed from the schoolmarm. All of her young life, Meg had been dealing with the prejudice of people like the schoolmarm, who didn't understand that Meg wanted to act and dress like a woman, but because of her situation in life, she dressed like a man. It wasn't a choice, but a necessity. And now it seemed as if that injustice was reflecting on Ruby.

With a toss of the hoe, Meg walked up to the teacher. "Okay, Miss Andrews, Ruby will no longer be attending your classroom. I'm sure that will make your life a little easier."

"Most definitely, since this is my fourth visit to your place this year. I'll have more time to spend on students who are not so...social."

Rage bristled Meg's insides, and her Irish temper roiled at the not so subtle reference to Ruby's antics. How dare the woman belittle her sister? Ruby could cause trouble, but still, she was a McKenzie, and Meg would protect her sister and the family name with her dying breath. "Maybe if your lessons weren't so boring, Ruby wouldn't be involved in seeking outside stimulation."

The woman gasped. "If your sister would study rather than spending her time kissing young men, then I wouldn't need to come out here. Good day, Meg."

Meg reached out and grabbed the woman's dress, her muddy hands clasping the material. It felt smooth and shiny and oh, so wonderful. The schoolmarm was in a hurry, and the material ripped, falling away from Meg's hands.

Oh, dear. She hadn't meant for that to happen; she'd

only wanted to feel the material.

"Get your dirty hands off my dress," the teacher said, taking a step back.

A smile lifted the corner of Meg's mouth. She'd been rude, but the woman had deserved it, though she hadn't meant to mar the lovely dress or the beautiful material.

Meg shouted after the woman, glad to see her leaving, "Hobble your lips about my sister, Miss Andrews. She's young, impressionable, and she's family. I won't have you trashing her good name. Now, get off my farm." She watched the woman hurry across the field to her buggy.

Ruby McKenzie could get in more trouble than a whole gaggle of small children. For some reason, she'd become fixated on boys and fornication and things she shouldn't. If she continued, Meg would have to speak to their father about finding her a husband. *Quickly.*

Meg strode to the quaint farmhouse, taking deep breaths to cool her temper at her youngest sister. The red hair and green eyes she'd inherited from her mother, as well as the Irish temper that went along with her disposition, were well known by her sisters. And right now, her stomach churned like a plunger in the butter crock at having to yet again deal with Ruby and her shenanigans.

Meg was the only one around to keep a rein on Ruby. Her mother had died, and her father was out trying to earn money for the family farm. Wouldn't it be wonderful to have parents who were present like other young women had? A family life, rather than three girls trying to make do. There was no one for her to turn to, but herself.

Ruby, Meg's beautiful, blonde haired, blue-eyed

sister with a pixie chin met Meg at the door, her expression contrite. "I can explain."

"What's to explain?" Meg asked, walking into the house and setting down her cowboy hat on an armoire. The house looked the same as the day her mother had died; only now, it was Meg's responsibility to keep it clean and tidy. "You've just been expelled from school for acting like a trollop."

"A trollop?" Ruby asked, a frown drawing her eyebrows together, as she rushed after Meg into the kitchen. "What's that?"

Annabelle, the middle sister and the only one in the family with dark chestnut curls with streaks of red and gold, hurried toward them. Annabelle was the peacemaker—the sister who kept the screaming arguments to a minimum and prevented Meg from killing Ruby on a weekly basis.

"A trollop is a woman with loose morals. A woman you don't associate with because of her reputation," Annabelle said in a calm, rational voice that lacked Meg's drama.

Annabelle was the quiet, soft-spoken one in the bunch. She seemed more refined, more of a lady than either Meg, who wore pants because of her chores, or Ruby, the beauty in the group.

"My morals aren't loose," Ruby said indignantly. She shrugged. "Those boys were stupid enough to pay me. I made well over a dollar today, charging them to kiss me and to—"

Over the last seven years, Meg had to learn how to interpret her sister's reactions. She'd had to learn what being a mother entailed. Though her own instincts were never as good as her mother's, Meg's intuition raised the hair on the back of her neck. What else had Ruby been charging for?

"What did you do?" Meg asked, knowing it couldn't be good. Her gut twisted with anger, and she wished for the thousandth time that her mother was still alive. Now that Ruby was older, Meg didn't know how to deal with her younger sister's knack for getting into trouble.

"It was nothing."

"What were you charging boys for?" Meg insisted, knowing there was something Ruby wasn't telling, and they were not moving until she found out.

"Oh, all right. I would kiss them on the lips for a nickel, and I would give them an open mouth kiss for a dime. Or if they were real adventurous, I would let them touch my breast for a quarter. Paid in cash up front," Ruby said, her blue eyes not flinching, not lowering like she felt shame.

Annabelle gasped, her brown eyes widening with disbelief. "Ruby Diane, how could you?"

Ruby shrugged.

"It was through my clothes. It's not like they could feel anything. All they felt was my dress," she said, like they were upset over nothing.

Good God, her mother was probably rolling over in her grave. Meg was out of her element. She needed her father here to help tame her wild youngest sister.

"Still you were charging them money, like a common whore," Meg said, knowing her mother would have taken a switch to her backside.

"You mean those women down at the saloon?" Ruby asked innocently. "Never. They felt my dress, nothing else."

Where had Meg gone wrong in teaching her youngest

sister? She'd tried to guide Ruby the same as their mother had taught Meg until she'd died when Meg was twelve and Ruby a mere eight years old

Meg shook her head. "It's morally wrong. The only man who can touch you is your husband, not silly schoolboys who will tell all the other little foolish boys. If this gets back to Papa…"

Tears welled up in Ruby's soft blue eyes. The same eyes their father had. "I only wanted to earn enough money to get Papa a birthday present."

Annabelle shook her head, her mahogany curls bouncing. "Letting boys kiss you and feel your breasts is not the way to earn money."

No, it wasn't, Meg thought, but how else did a woman earn money in today's world? There weren't many choices, and most women chose marriage over working drudgery jobs that paid them little.

Tears spilled over and slid down Ruby's cheeks, but her blue eyes glazed with defiance. "Boys are always asking me for a kiss, and I decided if they were stupid enough to pay me, then I'd give them their kiss and take their money."

"Oh, honey," Meg said, unable not to hug her youngest sister. Boys were stupid, and Ruby was a precocious young woman. And her tears got to Meg every time. "You're beautiful. Boys are going to chase you. I understand the satisfaction you must have felt to take their money, but you're playing with a prairie fire."

Ruby hiccupped a sob. "What do you mean?"

"Sometimes a boy can get so worked up by a woman's touch and her kiss that even when she's saying no, he keeps going. Why do you think Papa taught us all how to shoot? Why do you think we all carry a persuader hidden beneath our skirts?" Meg said, patting Ruby on the back.

"He said it was to protect us," Ruby replied, her blue eyes all innocent. "But why would anyone want to hurt us?"

God, this girl knew how to charm the rattlers off a snake. Meg knew the men would soon be coming around like bees swarming a hive. The honey was pure and sweet and so tempting. She needed her father's guidance in how to deal with her younger sister.

"Yes, and he's referring to men. He's trying to protect us from a man trying to take advantage of us and stealing our virtue."

"Virtue?" Ruby questioned.

Annabelle patted Ruby on the back. "A woman only has her good name and her virtue. Her virtue is her goodness, her purity, and her virginity."

Ruby leaned back out of Meg's arms and told Annabelle. "I'm still good."

The innocence of her statement caused Meg and Annabelle to laugh. "Yeah, we know that. But your future husband doesn't want to learn you were out selling your kisses in the schoolyard. He might think you were offering more than simple kisses."

Stepping out of Meg's arms, Ruby's brows drew together in a frown as she considered her sisters. "Seems to me if he was a good man, he wouldn't be out buying kisses and touches in the schoolyard, or he'd think I was a smart woman to trick all those boys into doing something so silly."

Meg drew air into her lungs and closed her eyes. Once her sisters were raised, married, and out of the house, she intended to live without any responsibilities, wear dresses, and sew pretty garments. This life was harsh, and becoming the head of the household at the age of twelve had stolen her girlhood from her. Soon, it would be her time to live. She promised herself every day...soon.

"Come on, it's time to put the chickens up before it gets dark," Meg said, ruffling Ruby's hair, like she was twelve again and not fifteen. "You've caused enough excitement for one day. Your punishment will be you have to clean the chicken coop, and you'll donate the money you earned to the house."

"No," Ruby whined, her blue eyes pleading with her sister. "Not the chicken coop."

Meg shook her head, knowing she had to be strong. "Sorry, I'm working in the garden, and it needs to be done. You're now home from school to help me."

"Lucky me," Ruby said.

"Should have thought of that before you kissed all those boys."

Ruby raised her head and stared at Meg, her sky blue eyes flashing defiance. "Next time I won't get caught."

Meg stopped. "Do you want me to tell Papa when he comes home?"

"No," she said sullenly.

"Then there won't be a next time." Meg questioned whether or not she'd been strict enough with Ruby. The girl had used her brains to come up with the one way she could earn extra money. Unfortunately, it could also damage her reputation. And if their Papa learned of her antics, she might be feeling the barber strap on her backside.

The three of them walked out the front door of the small house. "I'm not collecting the eggs tonight," Ruby said, flouncing alongside them. "That one hen bites me every time."

"It's my turn to collect the eggs," Annabelle said, walking quietly with them to the barn.

When Ruby got into trouble, Annabelle always went out of her way to make Ruby's life easier for a few days.

"I'll put up the goats," Ruby volunteered.

"Are those riders in the distance?" Annabelle asked, stopping and shading her eyes as she stared toward the horizon.

Meg strained her eyes against the setting sun. "Is that...? That's Papa."

"Papa," Ruby cried, running across the field toward their father.

"Something's not right," Meg said, gazing toward the two men on horseback. "He's slumped in the saddle. He's not sitting up straight and tall."

"Oh, my God," Annabelle said as she started to run. "He's hurt."

Meg's chest grew tight, squeezing the air from her lungs at the thought of something being wrong with their father.

*

Meg stopped and stared up at the man barely sitting in the saddle. "Papa, are you all right?"

His color was pale; his blue eyes were sunk back into his head and seemed dull. A scratch ran across his face.

"How're my girls?" he croaked through dry, parched lips.

"He's in a lot of pain. I got him home as soon as I could," the man on horseback said. "I'm Deke Culver. I was with him when he got hurt."

Emerald eyes gazed at Meg, his face covered with a

scruffy unshaven beard. Midnight black hair peeked from beneath his hat and matched his heavy brows. The man's lips turned up in a quirk of a smile.

"Good to meet you, Mr. Culver."

The girls walked silently beside their father until they reached the house.

"Let me help him down off his horse," Deke said, swinging his leg over his saddle and dropping to the ground.

The man was one tall, muscular jackeroo who wore his guns low across hips and moved with grace and speed as he hurried to her father's side.

He lifted their father off his horse and half carried him into the house. Annabelle went ahead of them, showing Deke where to take their father.

Meg turned to Ruby. "Go fetch Doc Henderson right now. Don't stop anywhere, just get him back here as soon as possible."

"Yes, ma'am," she said, her voice trembling. "Is he going to be okay?"

"I don't know," Meg said, fear rising like a wave of nausea, gripping her stomach in a vise. She hurried after Deke, who was helping their father climb into bed.

She didn't know where her Papa had found this cowboy, but thank God the man had been with him when Papa was injured. There was no way he could have made it home alone. It said a lot about Deke that he'd bring an injured man back to his family.

"Hi, my sweet Irish rose," her father said, as his hand reached for Meg's cheek.

Her lungs seized, restraining the sob that filled her throat. It was the name he'd called their mother. He thought she was their mom.

Deke glanced over at her. "What did he call you?"

She shook her head, unable to respond. "Papa, it's me, Meg. Where do you hurt?"

He closed his eyes. "So much I need to tell you."

"Ruby has gone for the doctor."

"Just let me rest for a bit, and then we'll talk," her father said his voice barely legible.

"I think he cracked his ribs. He's had trouble breathing," Deke said, stepping back to the door of the bedroom.

Annabelle pulled Papa's boots off and his dirty socks. With a warm washcloth, she gently bathed his face, wiping the dust from his fevered brow. "Would you mind taking his pants off for us?"

Deke glanced over at Annabelle, who turned beseeching hazel eyes on him. He sighed. "Sure."

They turned their backs while the cowboy removed Papa's pants and covered their father with a blanket on the bed.

"Thank you," Annabelle said with a smile as she began to unbutton his shirt.

Deke helped her pull the arms of the shirt off her father by raising him up in the bed. Papa groaned, the sound low and deep as they moved him.

Annabelle lifted the covers and looked at his chest. "Oh, my God, he's so bruised. What happened?"

Meg grabbed the coverlet and gazed at their father's black and blue torso. Her heart pounded, her vision blurring with unshed tears, as she stared at the damage to his chest and ribs.

The handsome, rugged man who'd brought him home shook his head and sighed. "We'd been working on a new case together. When James Rivera, our outlaw, suddenly left town, we chased him at full gallop. Your father's horse jumped a ravine, and somehow your father lost his footing in the saddle. He fell off the horse and tumbled down into the ravine. I stopped when I saw him fall." Deke looked at her father and then back at Meg. "Frankly, that first night I didn't think he'd make it. But he kept saying he had to get home. When he managed to tell me where he lived, I brought him here."

"Thank you, for bringing him to us." Meg stared at their father; his color was yellow, his breathing shallow. "When did this happen?"

"Two days ago. I'm surprised he made it this long. It was the least I could do. Your father's been good to me."

Meg stared at the shadow of the man her father was. He'd always been a big man, robust and healthy and strong. Sure, he'd been shot before. In his line of business, such were the injuries of the trade. Bounty hunting wasn't a safe occupation, but she'd never worried about his dying, before now.

"Do you think he's going to make it?" Meg asked.

Deke shook his head, his gaze on the man lying unconscious. "I'm not a doctor. I don't know. But I know he's hurt bad. He's been coughing up blood."

Oh, God, no, he couldn't die. Not her Papa.

She couldn't…she couldn't lose her beloved father. He was the one who took care of her. He couldn't leave her alone with Ruby and Annabelle. And Meg couldn't shoulder the burden of paying for the farm and putting food on their table. She couldn't take on one more thing. Placing her face in her hands, she felt Annabelle come up behind her and lay her hands on her shoulder. "We don't know anything yet. Let's wait for the doctor."

"I'm afraid. He's never been hurt like this before."

14

"I know," Annabelle said quietly.

Meg pulled her hands away from her face. She never let herself be vulnerable in front of her sisters. Never. Yet, the idea of losing their father and her having full responsibility was daunting. She loved her sisters, but she dreamed of her own life. Still, she knew as sure as her next breath that if something were to happen to their father, she'd take over the complete running of the farm and make sure her sisters had a home. They were family, and she'd care for them.

She gazed at her father lying still, his breathing shallow; she could almost believe he was a corpse. A scratch ran across his cheek, and a bruise marred his forehead. She'd never seen him look so frail.

The front door opened. "Meg, Annabelle? I have the doctor."

Ruby led the man into the bedroom. "Is he better?"

Meg shook her head. "Thanks for coming, Doc."

"Why don't you all clear the room and let me take a good look at my patient."

Meg and her sisters and even Deke left the doctor with their father. Outside the bedroom, Meg watched as they paced the floor of the quaint farmhouse, their shoes making a rhythmic thump on the wooden floor. Her mother had decorated the farmhouse with love, some antiques and homemade quilts and a wooden dining table. It wasn't fancy, but it was home.

Deke sat at the table, drumming his fingers. "Maybe I should go. I can spend the night in town."

"No, you brought our Papa home. You're welcome to sleep in the loft of the barn. There's a bed in there, and I promise you Ruby's going to fix us some supper just as soon the doctor leaves," Meg told him, feeling such a debt of gratitude toward this man. "Papa would want us to make certain you were treated well for your effort."

She watched Ruby flounce towards Mr. Culver and sighed. The girl was all fanciful with notions of love and poetry and men. Not the reality of the situation, which was working until you dropped with exhaustion. Ruby's head was cluttered with dreams that could only get her into trouble. Even now while their father lay hurt in the next room, she darted about the room like a butterfly seeking nectar.

"It's already cooked. We're having cornbread and stew tonight," Ruby told him. "I'm a very good cook, so you don't want to miss out on my stew."

Meg wanted to hit her. Did she never stop flirting? Was it just part of her nature like taking her next breath? If a man walked into the room, she automatically became a coquette. Where had she learned this behavior?

The bedroom door opened and the doctor walked out. "Why don't we all sit down for a moment."

Meg looked at his face and felt her stomach sink to her knees; her body shook so much she could barely stand. He had that fatherly-I've got bad news-expression on his face. She didn't want to see that expression; she didn't want to hear his news. It wasn't fair. She needed her father.

They sank down on the settee, the three sisters with the doctor sitting across from them in her mother's favorite rocker. Deke still sat at the table.

"Your father has suffered some serious internal injuries. His abdomen is swelling and filling with blood. One of his lungs has collapsed." The doctor paused and looked at each of them. "At this time, I don't think there's much hope."

Meg heard the words, but her brain refused to acknowledge what her eyes had already told her.

Ruby started to cry. "No."

The doctor sighed and ran his fingers through his hair. "I could be wrong. Sometimes these things fix themselves in a day or two, but more often the patient slowly slips away."

"No," Annabelle suddenly said. "No, he's going to get better. We'll take care of him. We'll take turns sitting with him and make sure he gets everything that he needs."

Meg's insides twisted into a hopeless knot of anxiety. She would do whatever was necessary to make sure her father lived. Living without her Papa was just not a choice.

The doctor smiled at her. "I hope so, Annabelle." He looked around the farmhouse. "I know you girls need your father. I'm going to leave now, but if you need anything else, just send for me. I left some laudanum by his bed. If he has pain, give him several drops."

Meg stood and wiped her sweaty palms on her pants. "Thanks for coming, Doc. We appreciate it." She glanced at her sisters, worried about them.

Ruby's face was white, her blue eyes wide and dazed like she was afraid. Annabelle sat on the couch in shock—her face pale, her hazel eyes almost ember, her lips pursed.

Ruby stood. "I'll see you out, Doc."

Meg watched her show him out, and once the door closed, Ruby started to cry. "We can't lose Papa. We just can't."

Annabelle rose and went to her along with Meg. "We'll do everything we can to keep him here with us."

17

Meg's heart rose in her throat, tears welling up inside her, threatening to spill. She refused to cry. But just like Ruby, she couldn't lose her Papa. She needed him.

*

The next morning Ruby ambled along on her way to the hen house to collect the eggs. She hated going to the chicken coop and fighting that crazy hen that liked to peck her. That chicken would soon be roasting in a pot if she had her way, but Meg said to wait until after spring when the new chicks would arrive. That bird might not make it until spring if she continued to peck Ruby's hands.

Ruby came around the corner of the barn, and her feet stopped, her mouth opened, and her breath seized in her throat. She stared in heated fascination as Deke swung an ax, chopping wood, naked from the waist up. The muscles in his back and chest rippled with strength with each swing of the ax. His skin was tanned, his muscles taut, and she wanted to run her fingers down his smooth skin. She wanted to know how a man felt without his shirt on. How he smelled after working hard.

"Good morning," Deke said, his emerald eyes staring at her, his breathing labored.

She licked her lips, her mouth suddenly dryer than a hot Texas summer day even though it was only March.

"Good morning," she said cheerfully, her heart racing, her mind slowing, and her eyes unable to move from the sight of his half naked body.

"Why are you doing that?" she asked, not really caring, but enjoying the view. Not wanting him to stop.

"I thought I would fill up your wood box for you before I left today, since your papa won't be able to chop for a while. How is he this morning?" He swung the ax.

18

At the crack of the wood splitting, Ruby felt her insides flutter. Good grief, this man was supple and strong as an ox. Yet, the mention of her Papa filled her with sadness. He looked so bad. "About the same. He keeps asking for my ma."

"When a man's hurting, sometimes his mind plays tricks on him. I know your mother's been dead for a while," he said.

"Yes, since I was eight," Ruby replied, wanting to keep him talking, yet wishing he would swing the ax again. She loved watching his muscles ripple across his back.

She smiled at him and batted her eyelashes, like she did the boys at school. "You said you're leaving today? Why?"

He leaned on the ax and studied her. "I need to get back to chasing down the criminal your pa and I were following. There's money on his head."

It wasn't working. Most boys were eating out of her hand when she smiled and batted her eyelashes at them, but Deke just looked at her. He was a man, not an addle-brained schoolboy.

"Do you have something in your eye?" he asked.

Good grief. The man was oblivious. "Why can't you wait until Papa can go with you? You should stay here with us until he gets well."

Deke sighed and shook his head. "Can't. Someone else could catch him by then."

The wind blew his hair across his forehead. He shivered. "I best get back to this. It's not exactly warm out here."

"Okay," she said just standing there ready to watch him.

"Don't you have some chores you need to do?" he asked.

The crunch of footsteps alerted Ruby that someone approached.

Annabelle walked up behind her. "Yes, the eggs need to be gathered. Go," she said, giving Ruby a little push.

Ruby knew exactly what her sister was doing. She was trying to get her away from this handsome cowboy. She'd laid eyes on Deke Culver first. He was her man. Maybe even her husband. "I'm going."

She hurried into the chicken coop and shoved the old hen out of the nest. She was going to get the eggs, and hopefully by the time she'd finished, Annabelle would have moved on, and then Ruby could talk to Deke some more. He was a man, not a boy, and she wanted to know what a man's kisses were like. Were they better than a boy's?

So far she was not too thrilled with the kisses she'd experienced from the schoolboys. They'd done nothing for her. She wondered what was the big deal about kissing? It was two sets of lips moving around. She'd felt nothing. No love. No lust. Mainly she'd felt disgust.

But a man... A grown man could definitely show her how kisses should feel and what all the poetry and excitement was about.

Finishing her chore, she walked out of the hen house and came to a stop. The wood was neatly stacked, and Deke was nowhere to be seen. She ran to the house, careful not to drop the eggs. He couldn't have left yet. He just couldn't have.

When she walked in the door, he was at the table eating breakfast. Annabelle stood beside him filling his coffee cup. "Anything else, Mr. Culver?"

"Thanks, you ladies have fed me very well."

"It's the least we could do for you after bringing our father home," Annabelle said.

"Ruby, go relieve Meg with Papa and let her come eat some breakfast."

She glared at Annabelle. She knew exactly what she was doing. She was keeping Ruby from Deke. She was trying not to let her get close to him, but Annabelle couldn't stop her. Deke was hers.

"All right, but I'll be back," she said and flounced away to the bedroom.

Softly, she opened the door and peered inside at Meg sitting beside her papa.

"You've got to pay..." A coughing spell took control of her father. Ruby watched as his face grimaced in pain. He gasped for air, his lungs wheezing. Blood gurgled from his lips, and Meg quickly wiped it away. "The bank. The mortgage is due in a month."

Ruby felt a pang of sadness overwhelm her. He looked so aged, his body badly bruised, his lips swollen.

Meg wiped a tear away from her eye, and Ruby felt her chest tighten. She'd never seen Meg cry.

"Do we have enough money in the bank?" she asked, and suddenly Ruby realized the perilous position they were in. Without Papa's income, their life could become very difficult.

"No. Somehow you're going to have to earn more. That's why I was chasing Rivera. We needed the money for the mortgage."

Meg sighed. "Oh, Papa."

"I...know...I'm sorry," he said. "Ask Mr. Clark at the bank for an extension. Tell him to give you thirty more days." His lids kept drifting down over his eyes, like he wanted to sleep.

"Papa, you can't die on me. We need you."

He smiled, his lids almost closed. "I know, baby. I know. I'm trying."

"Stay with me, Papa." She patted him on the arm.

His eyes closed completely. She reached over and checked his pulse.

Ruby stepped into the room, fear holding her in its grip, her heart no longer beating. "Is he…?"

Meg turned and looked at her. "No. Talking wears him out."

"Oh, thank goodness. You scared me for a moment." Ruby went and stood right beside the bed. "Annabelle said for me to relieve you and let you eat some breakfast."

"Thanks," Meg said slowly rising and stretching.

"Don't let Deke leave without me telling him goodbye," she said to her sister.

Meg frowned at her. "Why?"

"Just because I want to tell him goodbye and thank him for bringing Papa home."

Her sister studied her and then laid a hand on her shoulder. "You're not fooling anyone, Ruby. You're still playing with fire."

"I am not."

"I'm not arguing with you while our papa is lying in that bed. But you are not to be alone with Mr. Culver. Do you understand me?"

Why did they all treat her like she was a child? She was a woman. A fully-grown woman and she'd found herself a man. Mr. Culver would do very nicely compared to all those riff-raff boys from school. But he just had to wait until her Papa was doing better. "Oh, good grief. Go eat your breakfast."

Then Mr. Culver could court her and ask her papa's permission to marry her. She wasn't going to be stuck here on this farm for the rest of her life. But before anything could happen, her papa had to get well.

"Thank you, I will. But if I find you alone with Mr. Culver, you will be cleaning the chicken coop for the rest of your life."

Ruby felt her anger rise up in her like a volcano ready to spew, but she knew now was not the time to be fighting with her older sister. Meg thought she was the boss of everything. And if Papa died, she would be. A chill trickled down Ruby's spine at the idea of her oldest sister being in charge of everything and her Papa being gone. No, it couldn't happen. It just couldn't.

"All right. I promise not to be alone with him. Now, go eat," Ruby said, staring at her father's closed eyes, willing strength to him.

Ruby turned her back on her sister, sat in the chair next to her father, and said a quick prayer. She needed her papa. She needed him now more than ever.

"Come on, Papa. Don't die on me," she whispered.

Chapter Two

Annabelle watched as Deke rose from their breakfast table, the muscles in his arms flexing as he stood to leave. Dang, he was a handsome man and would make some woman a great husband. Could he be the man she dreamed of every night? Could he be the man who would sweep her off her feet and out of this place?

"Ladies, I hate to leave, but I should get on the road. This guy's already got a head start on me, and I want to find him."

Annabelle handed him a cloth sack. "I made you some hard tack for your journey and to say thank you for bringing Papa home."

Why didn't she feel something for this man? Ruby obviously felt some kind of attraction, and she was younger than Annabelle. Was there something wrong with Annabelle not to desire this handsome cowboy? She was lonely. She wanted a husband and a family of her own, not to live out her spinster years in this farmhouse.

"Thanks, Annabelle, I appreciate that." Deke took the sack from her hand, his lips curved up in a smile that didn't have her sighing with longing or blood rushing to her head. Was she not normal or had she not found the right man yet?

"When you catch the bastard, kill him," she said quietly. "Or at least make him suffer the way our father is hurting."

"Annabelle McKenzie! That's…" Meg's voice trailed off as Annabelle stared at her.

Their father was lying in the bedroom hurting, possibly dying, which would leave them without a man, without a decent way to make a living, without their beloved papa. Did Meg want Annabelle to wish him a nice trip to jail?

Deke touched her on the arm. "I won't make this easy on him."

"Thank you," Annabelle said, her hands twisting nervously.

This cowboy was well built and nice looking. She couldn't help but be envious of the way Ruby was able to openly express her desire for the man.

No man had ever courted Annabelle. Normally, she was the peacemaker between Meg and Ruby. Watching over their younger sister while Meg worked the fields and handled the animals, Annabelle had helped Meg run the family farm since their mother had died.

But for the last few weeks, Annabelle had felt a longing for more than just living here with her sisters, taking care of the farm and Ruby. A restlessness in her soul cried out and desired adventure.

She wanted anything besides remaining here in this house placating Meg and Ruby. She wanted a life of her own—the chance to meet a nice man, to be courted, to marry and raise a family.

"Leave a message with the sheriff about your father. Usually, I stop in several times a month to look at the wanted posters," Deke said, glancing at Meg.

"Will do," she said.

Now, the idea of slipping a ring on Deke's left hand and giving him a gaggle of children sounded like every young woman's dream—a farm and family of her own, a man to chase the loneliness away. But Annabelle felt nothing for Deke. Wasn't she supposed to know immediately he was the man for her?

If she was supposed to know at first meet, then none of the men in town were the one for her either. She didn't feel the urge to share her life with a single one of them. And absolutely none of them filled her with a longing of a physical kind. If anything, she felt revulsion for the men who walked the streets of Zenith.

Deke checked his gun holster, making sure it was tight, and picked up his hat. "Goodbye, ladies, I hope your father gets better."

Annabelle and Meg walked him to the door. "Goodbye, Deke."

Striding outside, he untied the reins of his saddled horse and stepped into the stirrups.

Ruby came running from the back. "Is he leaving?"

"Yes," Annabelle replied, wanting to stop her flirtatious sister as she grabbed a small tin off the table and hurried out the door after the handsome man.

"Deke, stop!" Ruby called.

He halted his horse and looked back at her. She ran up to him. "Here are some cookies I baked for you to eat on your journey. They're really good."

Annabelle stared at her younger sister as she smiled up at the handsome cowboy, her big blue eyes all doe-like and innocent. Why couldn't Annabelle be more like Ruby? Why couldn't she throw herself at a young man or flirt outlandishly? Instead, she hung back, waiting for her true love to find her.

Somehow, her true love must have gotten lost. She was almost eighteen, and he'd yet to show up.

"Thank you, Ruby." He took the tin of cookies and put them in his saddlebags. Once they were stored inside, he glanced down at her. "See you around, kid."

"Bye," she said, her voice a sweet sugary sound that made Annabelle want to gag.

She wanted to grab her younger sister and tell her not to be so flirtatious, so obvious. Annabelle was the middle one, the one most forgotten, and she wanted a man in her life just like the others.

Well, maybe Meg didn't want to marry. She never really said what she wanted in life.

Ruby turned around and strolled back to her sisters, a big smile on her young face. She glanced at them. "What? You're both staring at me like I was doing something wrong."

Meg shook her head at Ruby.

Annabelle turned toward the door. "He's too old for you."

"I'm fifteen."

"I'm seventeen," Annabelle said, walking back into the house. "I'm closer to his age."

"I saw him first," Ruby stated, hurrying up to Annabelle. "If anyone in this family is taking him, it's me!"

"And what would you do with him once you had him? Charge him a dime to kiss you?" Annabelle taunted, not sure why she felt the need to aggravate Ruby, but still feeling this urge to make her sister suffer. Ruby had no qualms about flirting outrageously with every man she met, and Annabelle wished she could be so blatant. Wished her one true love would come and rescue her.

"Enough," Meg suddenly commanded, clearly irritated with both of them. "Our father is lying in there gravely ill and you two are arguing over a man. Stop it this moment. We have to help Papa, not think about our own wants and needs."

Guilt seized Annabelle by the throat. Meg was right. Had being cooped up with her sisters warped her mind? Their papa lay in the next room ill, and she'd been dreaming of her forever-after, instead of thinking about how to take care of their father.

Meg gazed at them, her green eyes flashing with outrage, a look that Annabelle recognized from past experiences never meant well. "I'm going to go sit with Papa this morning, and then after lunch, Ruby you'll take over. Annabelle, you wash the dishes with Ruby. Plus, there are the animals to see to."

Things seemed so unsettled. When her father's broken body had come into the house, the air of change had swept through, tossing all of them about, leaving their futures unsettled.

Annabelle turned and made a face at Ruby, who rolled her eyes back at her. Annabelle started clearing the dishes off the table and putting them in the washtub. Most of the time, Annabelle kept Meg and Ruby from fighting, but today, Annabelle didn't want to get along with Ruby. Today, she ached with the need to put her younger sister in her place. To remind her that she had no business chasing after a man that much older than her.

Yes, their father lay in the next room, broken, battered, and she prayed unceasingly for his quick recovery. She wanted him to find her a husband, to walk her down the aisle. She needed her sisters by her side, but most of all, she longed for her papa to heal all the uncertainty.

"He's mine," Ruby whispered.

Annabelle cringed inside, knowing she should not respond, but unable to stop herself—not even really wanting this man, but somehow not wanting her sister to have him. Ruby was too young.

"I don't see a ring on his finger, so he belongs to no woman yet," Annabelle responded, her voice still its nice gentle tone with a current of steel running through it.

Ruby glanced at her. "Afraid of being an old maid like Miss Anderson?"

"No fears whatsoever, *child*." She reminded her sister, knowing Ruby thought she was a full-grown woman.

"I'm not a child."

"Just because you've grown breasts in the last six months, doesn't make you a woman," Annabelle whispered as she sank the dishes into the tub of soapy warm water.

"Not yet anyway," Ruby declared. "But I'm looking for a man to turn me into a woman, and Deke Culver looks like just the right sort of man."

Annabelle began to respond, but she heard a sob come from the bedroom. She listened for a moment and thought she heard it again. "Meg? Are you okay?"

Her older sister didn't answer.

An icy cold shiver traveled down Annabelle's spine, and her heart rushed up into her throat. She grabbed a dishtowel, rubbing her hands dry as she ran toward the bedroom. Time seemed to stop as she heard the sound of Meg sobbing. Meg never cried.

Fear gripping her, she reached the bedroom door with Ruby on her heels. Meg lay on the bed weeping. Annabelle glanced over and saw her father's eyes stared into some unknown world.

Her heart shattered as tears filled her throat with the realization that no longer would his Irish brogue fill the house with love and laughter. Never would he approve of her future husband or walk her down the aisle. Just that quickly, he was gone.

*

A week later, Meg drove the buggy into the yard of the farmhouse. She'd been to the bank to visit Mr. Clark and moved all the money from her father's account into her own. The money wasn't hers; it was for the farm.

She climbed out of the buggy and tied the horse to the hitching post outside the house. There were chores to do, supper to cook, and bad news to deliver.

Walking into the house, she glanced over at Annabelle and Ruby cooking supper over the potbelly stove. Since the day of her father's passing, as long as Deke's name had not been mentioned, they'd been civil to one another. If Deke's name came up in conversation, the claws were unsheathed and the fight was on. Yet, an uneasy silence permeated the house and left Meg longing to throw open the doors, open the windows, and air the place out.

"How did it go?" Annabelle asked, a black ribbon tied around her long curls in honor of their father.

They couldn't afford the proper grieving material, so the thin strips of satin in their hair had to do. Meg knew they all lamented the loss of their father and feared the future, but still it couldn't be healthy for the sad environment to continue.

"Have the animals been fed?" Meg asked, ignoring Annabelle's question.

In the strained atmosphere of the house, there was no laughter, no smiles, not even loud talking. They tiptoed around, as if they were too noisy, they'd wake up the dead. Almost as if they couldn't continue to live without being disrespectful to their father. She knew he wanted them to go on with their lives, but they had to learn how without him.

Yet, Meg didn't know if things would ever return to normal.

"I fed them," Ruby said, laying out the dishes and silverware on the table. "I even went ahead and put them up, since I thought you'd be tired when you came home."

"Thanks, Ruby, that was thoughtful." Meg stood, watching her sisters work together preparing supper, weariness overwhelming her.

She couldn't eat. She couldn't even stand the smell of food they were cooking.

This new world they found themselves in was different without their father here to oversee everything. Always before they'd been waiting for his return. No longer would he walk through the door, his boisterous laugh filling the house with love.

Now it was all up to Meg, and she didn't know what to do.

"We need to talk." She sank down onto a chair at the table and let the fatigue seep from her bones. She felt like she was a hundred years old, and yet she wouldn't be twenty for several more months.

Quickly, her sisters joined Meg around the table where the family had gathered for years to make decisions.

Meg took a deep breath. "Today at the bank, I moved the money out of Papa's account and into one with my name on it. That doesn't mean the money is mine, but ours. It was a total of one hundred and fifty dollars."

The girls smiled.

"Thank God," Ruby said, "I feared we would go hungry."

"Me too," Annabelle replied.

Meg shook her head. "It's not good news. The balloon payment on the house and land is due in less than thirty days. We need double that amount to make the payment and buy food."

"What did Papa do with his money?" Ruby asked.

Meg shrugged, times had always been tough, but in the last year a blown away barn and a late freeze had hurt their crops. Like a tide, money seemed to flow out, but never come back in.

"Papa spent more time around the farm and hadn't worked as much. That's why he went on this last trip. He needed money for the mortgage."

"How are we going to make that kind of cash in the next thirty days?" Annabelle asked, her face white as she grasped the reality of their situation.

"I don't have a clue," Meg responded, wondering if her own face had gone white when the banker had delivered the news. "And the bank is refusing to loan us more money or give us an extension. We must pay the loan in the next thirty days or lose our home."

Never one to sit still during a crisis, Annabelle jumped up and came back with a piece of clean paper and an ink quill.

"What are you doing?" Ruby asked, frowning at her sister like she'd lost her mind.

"I'm making a list of jobs for us to consider," Annabelle replied, gazing at her younger sister like she was a fool. "We can either lose the farm or go to work."

"Oh," Ruby said, and Meg could almost see the wheels of her mind working as she sat with her chin in her hands gazing at her two sisters. "We could sell baked goods to wranglers passing through town."

"Like we're letting you anywhere near those men," Annabelle replied, shaking her head but writing down the suggestion. "You'd be selling other goods."

"Hey, that's not fair," Ruby responded.

Meg held up her hand to silence the outburst. "This will mean not only working in town, but also our normal chores here at the farm."

As if there wasn't enough to do around the farm already, now they would be working in town for eight to ten hours. But if they lost the farm, Meg didn't know what they'd do.

Ruby frowned and glanced around the table at her sisters. "What kind of jobs can we get?"

"That's why we're making a list," Annabelle responded quietly.

"Everyone give me ideas for a job," Meg said, trying to keep them centered around how they could earn more money and not about the hopelessness of their situation.

"Saloon girl," Ruby said with a giggle.

"Do you know the duties of a saloon girl?" Meg asked. She knew Ruby said it in jest, but still it was time this girl got the fantasies out of her head and faced the realities of the situation. Being a calico queen could only be a harsh life. She didn't want her sisters in that situation.

Ruby stopped, her innocent eyes glancing at each of

her sisters. "Not really. I think she just hangs out with the cowboys who come in, and they buy her a drink or dinner."

Annabelle shook her head in disbelief and rolled her eyes.

Meg gazed at her youngest sister, who thought of herself as a woman but had no clue about real life. "It's time you knew the truth. A saloon girl does exactly what you said, but her wage is paid by the cowboys who take her upstairs and have sex with her. She is paid every time she allows some man to crawl between her legs and fornicate with her. She's subjected to disease and pregnancy. Is that the kind of life you want?"

"Ewww. No, that sounds dirty."

"Stay away from the saloon, Ruby. I know you're an innocent, but those men would take advantage of a young girl like you," Annabelle said quietly.

"I will. So that leaves us with, waitress, cook, housekeeper, and dressmaker," Ruby said, a frown on her beautiful face. "Like someone is going to hire us. We're the trouble making McKenzie girls."

So they were known around town as being unique—Meg because she wore men's clothing, Annabelle because she never let the mercantile man overcharge them, and Ruby because she liked to kiss boys. They each dealt with the realities of life the best way they could.

"Speak for yourself," Annabelle replied.

"Your turn, Annabelle," Meg said, ignoring them. Ever since Deke brought their father home, they had fought like two cats in a hen house. Never before had they sparred quite so much.

"She took all the jobs. The only thing I can think of is

accountant—like the bank would hire one of us to take care of their books," Annabelle said.

"There's always marriage," Meg acknowledged, watching the expressions on her sisters' faces. They often dreamed of a man who would sweep them off their feet, professing his love for them. But did life really happen like that? "Who are the eligible bachelors in the area? I know it doesn't sound ideal, but we're not bad looking. We don't have a dowry, but we've got a nice little farm. Surely some man would want to marry one of us."

"That's not going to get us a husband," Ruby replied. "They want a pretty woman who makes them feel like a man. Someone dependent on him for her every need."

Meg didn't know where Ruby got her ideas about what men wanted. She refused to believe that was what a man wanted in a woman. She wanted to think there was more, so much more, that a man looked for in his wife. "Well, I'm not donning a fancy dress or going to a saloon or batting my eyes at anyone."

"Who are the available bachelors?" Annabelle asked, twirling the quill in her fingers as she thought. "Ugh, there's Jimmy Brown, the hog farmer. I'd rather starve. He can't seem to quite get the pig smell off him."

Annabelle was ever the practical one. She always wanted a list to see what her options were before she made her decision. Yet, Meg feared the men that were here were slim pickings and a girl could do better looking outside of town.

Ruby smiled, "Don't forget Bill and Bobby Saunders, the twins."

"Oh, please, they aren't men. They're Mama's boys. I wouldn't marry them if they were the last available men in the state of Texas," Meg assured, shaking her head and gazing at Ruby like she'd lost her mind. "I can out shoot, out ride, and out smart them anytime."

Ruby shrugged. "Maybe that's a good thing."

"I refuse to take care of any man. He is either my equal, or he's not my husband," Meg replied. She'd raised two sisters; she wasn't raising a husband. She wanted a man who would treat her like an equal and was a man's man. Not a sissy. Someone like…Sheriff Zach Gillepsie.

"Who else," Annabelle asked. "Who's available that we would *want* to marry?"

"The banker's son, Joseph Clark," Meg said.

"He's a dandy." Annabelle quivered with revulsion, a grimace on her beautiful face.

"But you'd have *money*," Ruby responded, drawing out the last word. "I'll check him out."

"I just bet you will," Annabelle said softly.

"Hey, I'm your sister. You're supposed to be on my side."

"Yeah, I know," Annabelle mocked. "And you're crazy about boys. Don't you dream about love? About a man courting you and professing his undying love for you?"

"That's why I want a man. Not boys," Ruby snapped, her blue eyes flashing daggers at Annabelle. "And good luck finding any sod buster from around here that would profess his undying love for you."

"Stick to the plan," Meg reminded them, not really wanting to share the one name she'd thought about. She'd been thinking about him for a while now, but she seldom went into town, and when she did, she looked more like a man than a woman. Why would he be interested in her?

Annabelle looked down at the list. "I'm like Meg. I don't want any man I have to defend if there was a problem. Joey, as they call him, couldn't shoot to save his life."

"But his money could buy you security."

"I'd also have to sleep with him, and I'm not marrying a yellow belly," Annabelle said, giving Ruby a quelling look.

"Come on, girls, isn't there anything else we can do or someone we can marry?" Meg asked. "Is there no one on that list that interests either of you?"

Not that she wanted to marry them off, but they were down to the blanket in money, and she'd rather they had husbands than become a painted cat.

"There's that new sheriff, Zach Gillepsie. He's got a good job, and he's not half bad on the eyes," Annabelle suggested, raising her brows at Meg. "I saw you flirting with him in town last week."

Meg glanced at Annabelle. Yes, she'd flirted a little with Zach, and he'd seemed to reciprocate her attention. Would he consider marrying her and taking on her two sisters and herself?

Ruby raised her brows at Meg. "I didn't think you had it in you, Meg."

"Why? Because I dress like a man?" she growled, raising her voice in frustration. For being so smart, her youngest sister could say the stupidest things.

"No, I just wasn't sure you wanted a husband and children."

"And just when do you think I would have had the time or the opportunity to show I'm interested in courting? Deke is the only man who has come around here, except for Papa. I seldom go into town," she replied, her voice raised, and her eyes focused on her bratty sister. "I'm still a girl with dreams."

A hush fell over the table, and Meg sighed and waited a moment, trying to quell her frustration with her youngest sister. "What's the plan? Are we looking for husbands or getting jobs?"

"I'm looking for a job," Annabelle declared. "There's not a man on that list who's worth having, except for Zach, and you've got dibs on him. Maybe if Deke returns."

Annabelle turned her gaze on Ruby with a do-not-mess-with-me glare.

Ruby gave her a smirk. "Deke is mine."

"No ring," Annabelle reminded her.

Ruby raised her brows and gave her a haughty look. "Believe me, when I tell you I know just how to get Mr. Culver." She smiled a knowing sneer. "You don't stand a chance."

"You little witch!" Annabelle spat.

"Stop it, you two!" Meg exclaimed. "We're in serious trouble. Unless you want to make your living on your backs, then you need to pay attention and quit fighting over Deke. I doubt he would have either one of you."

Meg didn't know if that was true or not, but she was tired of listening to the two of them argue over a man she really didn't think was all that interested in either one of them. And they'd both acted like a fool over him the last time he was here. Poor man would probably never return.

"I'm keeping my options open on the men. There may be one who comes along I take a hankering to. But in the meantime, I'll see what kind of job I can get," Ruby said, turning her face away from Annabelle and speaking directly to Meg.

"Good. I'm going to find a job," Meg said.

"What about Zach?" Annabelle asked.

Zach was an unknown. Yes, he was a man she could consider tying herself to, but if he wasn't interested, then she'd need a back-up plan. Hell, maybe she needed both. All she knew for sure was she needed someone to help her save the farm.

"I'll talk to Zach and, if I get the feeling he might be interested, I'll ask him about marriage," Meg replied. "So all three of us are going to town tomorrow to find jobs."

"Looks like it," Annabelle confirmed, laying the quill down.

Ruby sighed and put her chin in her hand. "A job. I can't believe I'm going to work."

"And what a lovely little waitress you'll make." Annabelle teased her.

"I wouldn't be making fun of me. You might be the one with the waitress job, while I'm working at the mercantile or something more lucrative."

"I didn't know being a scullery maid was such a lucrative job."

"What's a scullery maid?"

"You clean and scour the floor, stoves, dishes."

"Ewww. It's bad enough doing that here. I hope I find something better," Ruby said.

They all laughed. It was good to hear laughter once again in the house. Papa was gone. They would always miss him just like they missed their mother, but for the first time in days, Meg felt more secure about the future. They had a plan. They had a focus. And now they could start working to pay off the bank.

*

Ruby couldn't believe she was working for one of the richest families in the town. Scrubbing floors and cleaning the outhouse wasn't what she dreamed of doing for the rest of her life. But there were times a girl had to help the family, and this was one of those times.

After her father's death, losing the farm would be like her parents dying all over again. In all of her life, she'd never felt so devastated as when her father had passed. She barely remembered her mother, and now her father was dead.

She wrung out the rags in the pail of water and once again applied the wet soapy cloth to the floor. On her hands and knees, she scrubbed the floor and hummed as she worked. Frankly, cleaning the outhouse could only be compared to scrubbing the chicken coop at home. And knowing Meg, Ruby would still be required to clean up after those nasty chickens. When she was rich with a family of her own, she'd never make her children do such horrible jobs. She'd never have a job cleaning outhouses and chicken coops.

"Hi," a deep male voice called from behind her.

She jumped at his greeting and then glanced up from her place on the floor. It was Clay Mullens, the owner's oldest son, a bachelor of approximately eighteen years of age. "You're new," he said, his brown eyes twinkling.

Tall with a dark curl of hair coming across his forehead, he was the type of man any girl would want. And suddenly Ruby wondered why she and her sisters had forgotten to put him on their list? Maybe because he was way out of their social range. His father was even richer than the banker. There was no way a Mullens' boy would find himself marrying one of the McKenzie girls.

She rose from the floor and curtsied. "Yes. My name

is Ruby."

He reached out to shake her hand, and she stepped back. "Oh no, I've been cleaning the floor. My hands are nasty."

He laughed and grabbed her hand. "Nice to meet you, Ruby. I'm not afraid of a little dirt."

His flesh felt warm and soft, and his smile had probably broken many hearts. Slowly, he released her hand. She couldn't help noticing the way his eyes were trained on her breasts, and for a moment, a nervous tremor went through her. She was being silly. He was just an immature boy who was curious about the female body.

She smiled at him. He was very nice on the eyes and had a pleasant smile and so far a nice personality.

"You don't look like you're old enough to be out of school," he commented.

"I finished this year," she said, feeling uncomfortable. If the news of how she'd been expelled got around, she could lose this job, and her sisters needed her pay.

"What about you?" she asked. "Are you in school?"

He sat down on the edge of the table in the kitchen. "I'm going back East to attend college this fall. Until then, I'm having fun."

"Sounds lovely," she responded, wishing her life were so simple.

"Not as lovely as you," he flirted.

"Why, thank you, kind sir," she responded, giving him her best coquettish smile. "I probably should get back to work before you get me fired."

"Oh, you're not getting fired. I'll make certain of that," he promised.

She heard his mother calling his name and watched as a frown appeared on his face. He glanced one more time at her.

"That's a summons from my mother, so I'd better respond." He stood and winked at her. "See you around."

She winked back at him. "Later."

Well, at least the scenery would be nice while she worked around here.

*

"Someday my dress designs will be in windows, and women will be ordering their wardrobe from me," Meg yelled and slammed the door. *Bitches!* The urge to take out her gun and pepper her initials in their wall was overwhelming, but she resisted.

Moisture welled up in her eyes, and she clenched her hands so tight her fingernails cut into her palms to keep the tears from falling. No tears. She refused to give in to this weakness here in the middle of Main Street.

Why could no one see the real Meg hidden inside? Why could they not see the woman she longed to become? Why did no one want to give her a chance?

She walked down the wooden sidewalk, her boots making clunking noises as she stomped away from the ladies' shop. They didn't believe she could sew. They didn't believe she had an eye for women's fashion. And yet, she couldn't argue with them. She didn't own a dress. Since she'd turned sixteen, she'd given up her only dress to Annabelle because it dragged in the mud when Meg worked around the farm. But that didn't mean she didn't long to wear pretty dresses and be considered a lady. That didn't mean she couldn't sketch a beautiful outfit, design the pattern, and then sew the dress, complete with lace tatting.

No, in this small town, her reputation for wearing pants had just kept her from getting a job. Even after the woman had seen Meg's dress designs, she'd still refused to hire Meg.

What if she didn't find any work? What would happen to them if they lost the farm?

She walked past the Chinese laundry. A "help wanted" sign sat in the window. Stopping, Meg plastered a smile on her face and entered the small establishment that smelled of starch and steam.

A man in what looked like white pajamas stared at her as she entered the building.

"You no wear dress?"

Good grief. Even in a Chinese laundry she had to answer questions as to why she didn't wear a dress.

She ignored his remark. "I'm looking for a job. I'm a seamstress. I can make repairs, sew buttons, sew clothes. Do you need help?"

"If you sew, why no wear dress?" he asked.

"Because I don't own one that fits," she responded, her voice raised as frustration grabbed her by the throat. God, she wanted to dress like a woman, really she did. But there were no funds for fancy clothes. And she could wear her Papa's pants without purchasing anything new.

He frowned at her and eyed her suspiciously. "Start tomorrow morning at eight. I pay you a nickel a piece."

"A nickel a piece? Not enough. I need at least a dime a piece."

"How do I know you sew? You start at nickel, and we'll see how you work out."

Meg frowned. She needed this job, and so far this was her only hope. "All right. I'll be here at eight in the morning. But once I prove I can sew, I'll expect a raise."

He shrugged. "Don't be late."

"Thank you." She walked out the door and hurried back toward the main part of town. A job. She'd gone from the pits of despair to at least being given a chance. Yet, he was paying her terrible wages. She would have to fix or repair one hundred pieces just to earn five dollars.

With a heavy heart, she walked toward her horse. This morning she'd let Annabelle and Ruby take the buggy while she'd ridden her horse into town. Getting them all to town on time every morning, plus doing their chores, was going to be a challenge. They had no choice, but to cope or face the consequences of losing the farm.

Passing the sheriff's office, she halted and peered in the window. Zach sat there writing in a notebook, his dark hair cropped short, his strong cheekbones held a shadow of stubble. She sighed as she peeked in the window at him. The sheriff was a muscular man who had her heart racing a little faster when she gazed at him.

No one else was in the calaboose. She stepped back and opened the door.

He glanced up from his paper and smiled. "Meg, good to see you."

"You too, Zach." Her heart did a little flutter when she looked at the handsome cowboy. His brawny body, warm smile and dark hair were enough to make a girl's tongue get all tied up in knots. Even Meg's tongue.

"I'm sorry to hear about your father." His big eyes darkened with sympathy, and she had the urge to fall into his arms and let him comfort her. But that was ridiculous. They hadn't even shared a kiss or done any courtin' whatsoever, and she wanted to fall into his arms? Hardly.

"Yes, it was so unexpected," she said, grief swelled up inside her at the thought of her papa, almost choking her with the ache. When would the pain become bearable? Every time she thought of him, it was like her chest squeezed, and she could feel tears forming. No tears. There could be no tears. "Do you have a moment?"

"Of course. Have a seat. Can I get you some water, something to drink? We don't have much here in the jail."

Sinking down into a wooden chair across from the big man, she tried to calm her rattled nerves. "No, I'm fine." She took a deep breath, trying to control her pounding heart. How do you begin to ask a man to marry you? How do you start? What do you say to persuade him to marry a pants-wearing woman with more responsibilities than she deserved at this stage in life?

He leaned back in his chair and considered her, his gaze leaving her warm and tingly.

"You've always been nice to me."

"Well, of course. A man would be crazy not to be nice to a pretty woman like yourself," he said, smiling at her, his earthy brown eyes twinkling, leaving her even more ruffled.

Meg did her best to return his smile. Maybe he was the answer to her prayers. "With Papa's death, it's just me and the girls living out at the farm. It's hard not to have a man in our lives."

Zach leaned forward. "Meg, any time you need help, let me know. I'll do whatever I can to help you girls out. It's the least I can do. Your dad was a good man."

"Thanks." Meg wondered if she should use some of the tactics her youngest sister utilized—flash her eyes at him, flirt, and put a pout on her lips—but that was just weird. It made her cringe when she thought of pulling a Ruby stunt. Yet, they worked for her youngest sister.

"The girls and I would love for you to come to dinner," she said, twisting her hands in her lap, more nervous than a bride on her wedding night.

"That would be nice. I get tired of eating my own cooking or what's served at the restaurant. I'd love some home cooking."

She didn't know how to flirt and bat her eyes at a man. She didn't know how to be coy and seductive. She didn't play cat and mouse games with anyone. She was a straight shooter. A woman who told you like it was, and if you didn't want to play, then get out of the way. She didn't know how to play flirtatious games.

Nerves gripped her insides like a dog with a meaty bone. "Look, I'm not good at this flirting stuff. You're nice to me, and I hope it's more than just being friendly." She paused and then took the plunge. "I need a husband. And you were my first choice."

His brows rose and he stared her, his face almost frozen in place.

Oh, God, she was making a fool of herself. She was halfway in; she might as well look like a complete old maid desperate for a man.

"I don't know if you're wanting to get married, but I like you. I'm not a woman who needs hearts and flowers. Just a good honest man who wants to spend the rest of his life with me and raise a family. Of course, you'd also be taking on my sisters until they marry. I'm not hard to get along with. But I expect total honesty, no drinking, and I need some help with the farm. So what do you think?"

The man's mouth opened, but nothing came out. Finally, he shut his lips and swallowed. "Can I think about it and get back to you?" He stumbled. "This—this is kind of sudden. How soon do you need to know?"

Meg shrugged. "Pretty quickly. We've got the farm, and I need some help there."

She wasn't going to tell him about the mortgage until he'd agreed to join her herd. Then he could join forces and work toward saving the farm.

"I don't want a big wedding. It would probably be just the two of us and my sisters. And anyone you'd like to invite, of course," she said, nervously wringing her hands in her lap, her stomach churning with the urge to throw up.

"Of course." Sitting back, he contemplated her across his desk.

He didn't say anything, and an awkward silence filled the room. She licked her lips as anxiety tightened its hold on her stomach, until she feared she would puke right there in his office.

"Well, I better let you get back to work. You think about it and let me know," she said, rising from the chair.

"I'll do that." His response was curt and to the point. He rose and acted like he would walk her to the door.

She walked to his side and thinking of Ruby, she told herself to act boldly. She reached up and kissed him on the lips. It was just a peck, an awkward brush of her lips against his, but still it was the beginning. It wasn't bad for a first kiss. His brows rose and when she released his lips, his mouth opened like he was going to say something, but nothing came out.

Okay, so maybe most women didn't make the first move, but if he was truly interested in being with her, they needed to skip a few steps and go right to the courting stage. After all, they could be standing in front of a sin-buster, saying their vows any day now.

She leaned back from him. "Please, can we keep this our little secret for now?"

If the town gossips found out about her marriage proposal, they would be going from house to house with her scandalous proposition. She'd never live the ridicule down and would never have another marriage proposal in this small town.

He held up his right palm as if he were swearing to tell the truth. "Sure. No one needs to know."

She smiled at him and placed her hand on his arm.

"Later, sheriff," she said and hurried out the door.

God, she hoped she hadn't just made a complete ass out of herself.

Chapter Three

A week passed with Meg working eight hours during the day at the laundry and then taking pieces of the mending home with her to work on at night. In seven days, she'd completed seventy pieces, and slowly the stack of work was going down. She had at least another weeks worth of work before she'd be caught up and could handle the pieces as they came in.

Before she went home, she had an important question for her boss. "Cho Linn, when are you going to pay me?"

The man's face grew serious, his dark eyes cold. He waved his hand away. "Not today. Not this week."

"So when?" she asked.

"When you finish."

"But I need money now."

"Not now."

Meg gazed at the man, her Irish temper flaring inside like kindling on a fire. "Don't think you can double cross me. I will get my pay."

"Next week, next week," he said. "Now go home."

She gave him one last glare and then walked out the door. She still had to pick up Annabelle and Ruby, and then there were chores to do.

Hunger gnawed at her stomach, reminding her she'd

not eaten today. Seldom did she eat lunch, and supper had been lean the last few nights. They were living off the eggs and the chickens, and they wouldn't last forever. Their hen house was on the small side, and though the eggs were lovely, occasionally they killed a hen just to get meat. They craved meat, but eventually, the hens would run out. Then what would they eat?

Tonight, Zach was coming to dinner. All Meg could think to do was to kill one of her laying chickens. They needed something in their diet besides eggs.

Meg walked down the alley to where the horse and buggy were tied. The smell of burning applewood tempted her nose, and she breathed in deeply, remembering how her father used to smoke hams and turkeys. Sometimes, he'd use mesquite, and sometimes, he'd use applewood, but no matter what he used, the meat always tasted flavorful.

A pang of grief gripped her chest, and she gasped to keep from doubling over in pain at the memory of her father. They'd lost so much when he'd passed. Now they had no one.

Ambling down the alley, she wasn't paying attention until she realized she was standing and watching a ham turning on a spit over a fire pit. She was hungry. She was starving. She was sick of eggs, and there was a roasting ham, the smell radiating through the air like a beacon for beggars.

Thank God, it was too hot for her to take because she didn't think she had the strength to resist. Except, a second ham lay wrapped and cooling on the table. These people had two hams. Two and she needed one to feed her sisters. Just one to keep them from starving. One to serve to Zach at dinner tonight.

She glanced down the alley; there was no one around. Quickly, she yanked the ham off the table and ran as fast as she could down the path. She'd never stolen anything in her life. Surely, she could be forgiven just this once.

*

Annabelle glanced around the crowded restaurant and sighed. Today was her third day working in the Rusty Café. She'd never eaten here before and after witnessing the dirty kitchen, she never would. No, it wasn't the best work, but it was a paying job. And they needed the money.

"Order up," Rusty yelled from the back.

Annabelle hurried through the tables toward the kitchen. Rusty's wife handed her the two plates.

"Get 'em out there before they get cold," Georgina told her brusquely. The woman was less than friendly and even appeared downright rude most of the time.

"Yes, ma'am," Annabelle replied, her feet already moving toward the table whose order she held. It was a job. A way to help save their family farm, and she could put up with just about anything as long as she made some money.

Leaning over to place the plates in front of a cowboy, she felt his hand on her butt. She tensed and had to remind herself not to dump his lunch over the top of his head.

"Thanks, darling."

She glared at him and smiled, her voice steely. "Sir, if you don't want your lunch in your lap, I would recommend you remove your hand immediately." She stared at him her look colder than a Montana blizzard. "This isn't the saloon."

He dropped his hand. "Sorry, you're so young and

sweet looking. You're hard to resist."

"That's not the way to win my heart," she commanded, setting the plates down. "Anything else, gentleman?"

"Nope, I think that will do," the groper replied, giving her a warm smile she wanted to scratch off his face.

"Good. Enjoy your meal."

She hurried off to see if the next table's order was ready and then to see to some new arrivals. The work was non-stop during the breakfast, lunch, and supper hour. In fact, her sisters had waited for her at least twice this week. So far, it was a job, nothing more.

During lunch, it was non-stop, and then afterwards there was always something they had for her to do. Sometimes, Annabelle wondered if letting go of the farm wouldn't have been easier. They could have gone somewhere new and had a fresh start.

"Annabelle, get in here," Rusty, the owner called.

She went into the kitchen.

"Hey, love, would you mind taking out that trash there?"

"Sure," she replied. "Watch and don't let table four leave without paying."

"Okay," he said, grinning.

She bent over to pick up the bucket of trash and felt him lift her skirt. A large warm hand massaged her butt. What was it with the men in this restaurant? Did they just think she was available for them to grope?

She whirled around and almost threw the trash bucket at him. She dropped it to the floor. "Stop! Get your hands off me!"

He smiled. "Oh, honey." He winked. "You enjoy it. I

know you do."

The urge to lift her skirt and pull out her shootin' iron, had her fingers twitchin'. She would certainly enjoy watching him dance to the sound of her bullets.

"No, I do not enjoy your hands on my ass. Keep them to yourself," she scolded firmly and picked up the trash facing him. From now on, she'd be watching Rusty. She wouldn't turn her back on him again.

When she came back inside from emptying the trash, he yelled, "Table three's order is up."

He smiled at her and blew her a kiss when she picked up the order. She scowled at him.

Her feet were killing her, and the lunch rush usually lasted at least two hours. She still had another hour before she could sit down and count her tips. And then when she arrived home, the smell of food would linger on her clothes and she couldn't stomach the thought of eating. Two weeks in, and she was beginning to hate this job.

"Lady," some man yelled. "My coffee cup has been empty for the last twenty minutes."

What an exaggeration. "I'm coming your way."

A woman sat in the corner watching her. Well dressed in the latest women's fashions, she almost seemed too fancy to be in a restaurant like this. A hat sat jauntily on the top of her head; her cheeks and lips were a brilliant red.

After Annabelle had given the man his coffee, she walked over to the fancy woman's table. "What can I get for you today? The specials are roast beef—"

"Honey, I don't eat in this establishment." She laid a card on the table and pushed it toward Annabelle. "You're quite beautiful. You could be earning a lot more money."

"Uh, thank you," Annabelle said, feeling confused. If the woman was a calico queen just like she thought, then what was she doing here talking to Annabelle?

She laughed. "I bet you're still as innocent as the day you were born."

A blush crept up Annabelle's face, and she didn't know how to respond to the woman. Who was she?

"I just stopped in here because I heard the boys talking about Rusty's new hired help. When you get tired of being paid nothing, being groped by the scalawags in this establishment, then contact me. The hours are longer, but the pay is much better."

Annabelle picked up her card and gasped. The woman ran the Happy Days Brothel. Catering to a man's pleasures, the card said, and Annabelle felt her heart leap into her throat.

She stared at the woman in surprise. Annabelle's image of a prostitute didn't match the woman's appearance.

The woman laughed. "Yes, you're an innocent. You know we could use that to your advantage. We could sell your virginity. You'd bring in top dollar."

Oh, my God. The woman wanted Annabelle to sell her virginity? Really? They were certainly desperate, but she wasn't ready to earn her living on her back. Not yet anyway.

"I'm not interested," Annabelle spat out. Her mouth felt like it was filled with dust.

"I understand, but keep my card just in case you get enough of being a waitress." She rose from the table and smiled at her. "Good day, Annabelle. Come see me."

Annabelle watched the woman walk out the door, her

head held high, wearing the latest fashion and looking so regal, while Annabelle wore food stains and smelled of today's special.

A shiver shimmied down her spine and left her feeling rattled. She glanced around at the packed dining hall. She certainly didn't want to do this for the rest of her life.

"Order up," Rusty called, pointing at her to get over to the kitchen. She hurried across the room.

Picking up the plates, her arms loaded down, she smiled as she placed them in front of the diners. They all stared at her. For once, she felt like she was part of the daily special and revulsion filled the pit of her stomach, leaving her nauseous. God, she was coming to believe that being a saloon girl could not be any worse than a waitress, except for that final detail. Having sex with men who were not her husband and she didn't even know their name would be like spreading your legs on a buffet, only she'd be the main course.

But being a waitress was not any easier. The men gawked at her like they imagined she was naked. Twice now she'd threatened to pour a man's lunch in his lap if he didn't remove his hand from her person, and then there was Rusty.

God, she hated this job. She hated it with a passion, but hopefully, it was temporary. But without Papa bringing home money, how could she and her sisters keep up the mortgage on the farm? And at what cost to their lives?

*

Meg ran around straightening everything, making sure the house looked just right. Her sisters had helped cook the side dishes and set the table. They all knew this was a big night. They had been shocked when she'd unwrapped the ham.

"What time is he arriving?" Ruby asked.

"He promised he'd be here at six."

Annabelle glanced over at Meg. "Where did you get the ham?"

Meg bit her lip; she hated lying, but knew she had to, or her sisters would refuse to eat the meat, and they needed the energy the ham would give them. "Someone paid Ho Chinn with the ham, and he doesn't eat pork."

"Oh, well, thank goodness, he doesn't like pork," Annabelle said, slicing up the meat and laying it on a plate. She turned from the stove. "You're not wearing those pants, are you?"

"This is all I have," Meg said, wanting to kick her sister for such a stupid statement. Didn't they realize she'd let the two of them have any material, any chance at new clothes? She'd done without, so they could wear dresses and have new shoes.

"Come with me," Annabelle commanded. "The least we can do is change your shirt and put some lace on the collar."

Meg followed her into the bedroom she shared with Ruby. So far, none of them had moved into their parent's bedroom. It just didn't feel right. They had closed the door on the room, unable to see where their father had died.

"Here," Annabelle instructed, handing Meg a flowery shirt. "Put it on."

Meg slipped it on and tucked the tail into her pants. So now, instead of plaid, she was wearing a tight floral shirt with her pants.

Ruby followed them into the room. "Sit down and I'll

fix your hair."

While the hair iron warmed up on the fire, Ruby took down Meg's red hair and brushed out the ponytail she always wore. "You know if you fixed yourself up a little more you'd probably be the prettiest one of us."

"And just when do you think I'm going to have time to do all this primping? Are you going to get up early to feed and water the cattle?"

Sometimes she didn't think her sisters realized how much she sacrificed for them. Sometimes she didn't think they knew how much work she did. Sometimes she didn't think they realized she was only a couple years older than either one of them.

Annabelle laughed. "She can't even take care of the chickens."

"Hey, I'm about to fix her hair. I would recommend the two of you be a little nicer."

Meg gazed at her in the mirror. "Don't ruin my hair. Tonight is very important to all of us, unless you want to spend the rest of your days on your hands and knees scrubbing floors."

Nerves filled her, and she couldn't help but wonder if he would accept her offer to be her husband. This time next week, she could be married, and he could be living here with them.

Ruby took the comb and parted Meg's hair. "No, thank you. That ole woman is a witch. I never get them clean enough for her." She put the hot curling iron in Meg's long hair and twisted it around the iron barrel.

Meg stared in amazement as her sister transformed Meg's wavy hair into soft curls.

When she finished, Ruby stepped back. "I knew there was a beauty underneath that hat and jeans."

"Wow!" Annabelle declared. "You're so pretty. If this man doesn't ask you to marry him, he's just plain stupid."

Meg stared in the mirror at her reflection and was amazed at the transformation. She did look pretty; even with her pants on, she looked like a woman. She wanted to be like all the other women she'd known.

"There's one thing missing," Meg exclaimed. She reached into the pocket of her jeans and pulled out her secret desire. She'd loved lipstick since she was a young woman and found a pot of the paint. Since then, she'd secretly put the color on her lips when she didn't think people would notice.

"Meg?" Annabelle said. "That's what a painted cat uses."

Ruby started laughing. "Are you saying our sister is a prostitute?"

"Oh, please. I can't wear dresses or look nice. Why can't I have one little vice? Don't you think I deserve something that makes me feel like a woman?" Meg said, sick to death of being the responsible self-sacrificing sister. Why couldn't she look pretty and have a man courting her?

For a moment, neither sister said anything.

"It's just a pot of rouge."

"Oh, all right," Annabelle conceded. "I guess it can't hurt."

"Show me how to put it on?" Ruby said, watching Meg dab her finger in the pot and smear the color across her lips.

"The secret is to get it so light no one notices," Meg said as she dabbed the paint on, evening out the color. It was the first time in weeks the sisters had enjoyed a moment of being women in each other's company.

Meg realized how much she missed the camaraderie between the three of them and hoped things would soon return to normal.

"Wow. I can't wait to try it," Ruby said, almost jumping up and down like a little kid.

"Annabelle, here you need some color on your lips." Meg smeared a dab of the color on Annabelle's lips, and she gazed at herself in the mirror. "Just that little touch of color adds so much."

"Don't forget me!" Ruby squealed.

"How could we ever forget you?" Meg said with a laugh. She rubbed the paint across her youngest sister's lips.

Ruby pranced in front of the mirror, making a kissing pout with her mouth and batting her eyelashes.

"Now, look what you've done. You've given her even more weapons to use on boys."

Ruby smiled at Annabelle. "Don't be jealous. I'm just adding to my arsenal, so some young man out there will be unable to resist my charms."

Meg and Annabelle laughed. "Where does she get this stuff?"

Annabelle shook her head. "I don't know."

A knock on the front door interrupted their fun, and Meg felt her insides twist into a knot. This was it. "Oh dear, he's here."

Taking a deep breath, Meg tried to calm her nerves. This night was so important and could decide if they kept or lost the farm. If he said yes, it would be easy, but if he said no, she'd be adrift, lost not knowing what to do.

"Let's go have dinner with our guest," Meg said, and they walked out of the bedroom together.

With a shaking hand, Meg threw open the front door, and Zach's mouth dropped like a boulder falling off the edge of the canyon floor.

"Wow, you look...fine as cream gravy, only more stunning," he said, standing there.

"Thank you." She took him by the arm and escorted him into the house. "You're not too bad looking yourself, cowboy."

The shirt he wore matched the earthy brown tone of his eyes, and she couldn't help but notice the snugness of his pants. His body was trim, tight, and lean. And she wondered what a wedding night would be like with Zach.

Annabelle stepped up beside Zach. "Here, let me take your hat."

"I can show you where you can wash up," Ruby said as she took him by the arm and led him into their parents' bedroom where a pitcher of water and a towel waited on the butternut washstand. "As soon as you're finished, we'll have dinner," she added before closing the door.

Meg shook her head at her sisters. "Poor man."

They giggled.

These two would certainly keep any man Meg contemplated marrying on the matrimony road of integrity. She knew what they carried beneath their skirts, and those little persuaders carried enough kick to make any man sit up and take notice. One shot would be all that was necessary to get him back in line.

"He's handsome," Ruby exclaimed with a grin on her face.

"A sheriff's wife. I think that fits you," Annabelle said with a smile. "I made a buttermilk pie for dessert."

Meg stared at her sisters. Sure, there were times she

wanted to strangle her two siblings for their constant nagging and fighting, but then there were times when she didn't know how she could live without them. They were always there for her. They were her family.

"Thanks, girls. This means a lot," Meg said.

Zach came out of their parent's bedroom, holding up his hands like a two year old. "I washed up."

"Let's eat," Meg announced.

He pulled out her chair, and she sat at the end of the table. "Please, Zach, you're our guest of honor. You sit in Papa's place."

He frowned, but he pulled out the chair she gestured at and sank down.

"How about a slice of ham?" Annabelle invited.

"Thank you."

Ruby smiled at him. "Annabelle baked a buttermilk pie for tonight. We haven't had pie in ages. She hates to use all the eggs for pies."

Meg frowned at her sister. He didn't need to know how desperate they really were. He didn't need to know how much they needed a man who could make a living for them.

She cut into the ham and took the first bite. It was succulent and moist, and she had to chew extra hard when she thought of how she'd acquired the meat. Someday she'd repay the Moore's for the stolen property. Someday she'd have enough money that she wasn't worried about starving. Someday she'd earn enough money from her dressmaking designs to live a good life.

Zach took a bite of his ham. "Where did you get this ham? This tastes really good."

"It was given to me." For a moment, Meg almost

choked on the lie she'd told.

"Ho Chinn gave it to Meg," Annabelle said.

"He's not far from the Moore's, is he?"

"His business is about three doors down," Meg said reluctantly, not really wanting to confirm what she could see were suspicions forming in his mind.

Zach stared at Meg, and guilt washed over her, causing her insides to cringe with the knowledge that he knew. God, she hoped it didn't show on her face. She was serving the sheriff a stolen ham. Could she go to jail?

Zach stared with disbelief at Meg, his forehead in a crinkle like he didn't quite understand. "Tom Moore is known for his smoked hams and turkeys. This tastes so much like what he sells." He paused and shook his head "He reported one stolen today. Said he stepped into the house to get another ham, and when he came back, the one he'd left cooling was gone."

Meg swallowed and smiled. Her food sat like a rock in her belly as cramps rippled from her intestines. "Oh, no. I hope he finds out who took it."

Zach laughed and stared at Meg, his brown eyes knowing. "Ho Chinn doesn't give anything away. I think I know who took the ham, and they won't be taking another one, will they?"

Meg tried to smile, but her face felt stiff. Her lips refused to work, and her tongue felt glued to the roof of her mouth. Oh, God, he knew she'd stolen the ham, and now her sisters would know of her thievery.

Annabelle looked at Zach and then at Meg. "Meg McKenzie, what is he saying?"

"You didn't get this ham from Ho Chinn, did you?" Zach asked.

"Please tell me we're not eating stolen food," Annabelle declared.

Meg looked at her sisters and then at Zach. She sighed, closed her eyes and confessed. "We were hungry. Ho Chinn hasn't paid me yet, and I didn't want to fry up another hen tonight."

Ruby threw down her fork, making a clattering noise on the plate. "Papa would not have approved. I think you need to take the rest of this ham back where it belongs," she said quietly. "You took my money away from me when I'd done wrong. You need to pay for the ham." She pushed her plate back, like she was done.

Annabelle did the same, and they stared at Meg like she'd robbed a bank. What could she say? She'd been starving, worried they weren't getting enough to eat, and desperate enough she'd taken what she needed at the time. It was her duty to take care of her sisters, and she was failing miserably.

Zach looked at her sisters and then at Meg. "Ladies, there is no sense in this good food going to waste. I'll talk to Tom tomorrow and see if we can set up some kind of payment arrangement. I'm sure Meg won't steal again, will you?"

There was a long moment of silence, as Meg sat there trying to decide if she would steal food again. What if they were hungry? With her working from early morning to dark and not receiving her paycheck, there was no way she could hunt or fish to put food on the table. She had so few options, and none of them included letting her sisters go hungry.

There were only so many chickens out in the yard she could kill before they lost their eggs and the meat. She was working as hard as she could to feed them all, but it wasn't enough.

Laying her fork down, she glanced at Zach and then at the girls. "If I could earn a decent wage and get paid, there wouldn't be a need to steal food. No need for us to all work at menial jobs, where we were treated less than respectably by our employers. You're a man. You earn a decent living. You don't know the feeling of going hungry."

Zach stared down at his plate. "No, I don't. But I believe in right and wrong, and stealing is wrong. Are you that desperate?"

Meg immediately jumped in. "Of course not. We just can't find decent jobs that pay enough. I've been working for Ho Chinn for over a week, and I've yet to receive my money. If I could earn the same salary as most men, then there wouldn't be a problem."

Zach picked up his fork and took a bite of the ham. "Is that why you wear men's pants? Trying to be a man and earn a decent living?"

Meg felt her stomach clench. Maybe she should just put up a wanted poster—the first man who bought her a dress won a complimentary steak dinner for two. She couldn't allow her frustration with this question to reflect in her tone, but she was getting damn tired of repeating herself. "I wear men's pants because a dress drags you down when you're out trying to plow the garden or chase the cows or tame a horse. Skirts get in the way and can get you killed. I'm not ready to die."

They all stared at him like they'd reached an impasse in the meal. The sisters couldn't get past Meg stealing their food; he couldn't get past Meg's pants, and she was suddenly thinking everything was lost. Why would he want to marry a woman who wore pants and stole hams?

He looked around the table at the women gathered there. "You girls are on the hunt for a husband."

"Of course not," Annabelle scolded.

"What?" Ruby said, acting stunned. "I'm too young."

"You know I am," Meg replied, staring him in the eye. She was not backing down. "I need someone to help me with the farm. Someone who's willing to take on part of the responsibilities. Someone who will bring in some cash."

If he had a problem with what she'd said, then he shouldn't have come tonight. He shouldn't be here.

Zach picked up his glass of water and glanced at Annabelle. "Let's have that pie you were talking about. Then Meg and I will go for a stroll."

Annabelle smiled at him. "Coming right up, Sheriff."

*

They stepped outside, and Meg glanced up at the stars shining overhead. A big round butterball of a moon stared back at her.

Zach took her arm and placed it in the crook of his. They walked out into the yard where the cloudless sky shone brightly with stars and the coyotes howled with their prairie tenor. "I've never been around women like you girls."

"What do you mean?"

"I have four brothers. The youngest one is a bit of a troublemaker. You girls seem to get along."

Meg started to laugh. "No, not always. They were on their best behavior tonight."

"Tell me, Meg, do you find me attractive?"

She stopped and stared at him in surprise. Didn't he understand that's why she'd chosen him instead of some other cowboy? Did he think she'd have chosen just any man?

"That's why I asked you to dinner. You were the only man in town I would have considered."

"And what happens if I say no?" he asked.

She gazed at him, her stomach falling to her feet. "I...I don't know. There's no one else from town. I may have to consider a mail-order husband."

Zach smiled at her and brushed the hair away from her face. "You're beautiful."

"Nah," she said, turning her face away. "I'm just a woman stuck wearing pants."

"Does that bother you?"

"More than you'll ever know," she said, her voice whisper soft. "So, are you attracted to me?" she asked, thinking it was only fair to ask him the same question.

"Yes, I am," he whispered.

His face was inches from hers. He was so close she could see the way his eyes flickered in the moonlight. Her heart was galloping like a runaway horse. Her lungs felt like they were being squeezed, and her face burned where his fingers had touched her skin. She watched as his lips lowered toward her own.

She tilted her face up, eager to meet him halfway, wanting, needing this kiss like her next breath. His lips covered hers, and he pulled her up against him, smashing her breasts into his chest. He tasted of sweet buttermilk pie and moonlit madness.

His lips devoured hers, his tongue running along the edge of her mouth. She'd expected to feel revulsion since she'd never been kissed before, but no, there was enough sizzle in this man's lips to have her craving for something she couldn't define. She didn't want to stop. She didn't want him to cease what he'd started.

He broke off the kiss, and she moved closer, wanting more, not ready for this to end. When she opened her eyes, he was staring down at her. "I think I better go."

"Oh," she said, startled he was leaving so soon. They'd just walked out the door. He hadn't told her yet if he wanted to marry her, and she needed an answer. She had to know.

He tilted her chin up and brushed his lips against hers once more. "Don't be stealing anymore hams."

She stepped back and shook her head. "I won't. I'll take it back tomorrow morning."

"Keep it. I'll pay for it as long as you promise you won't steal again."

She sighed. "Thanks. It's pretty sad when you have to buy your own dinner."

He laughed. "No. Dinner was good. The stolen ham was excellent, the vegetables wonderful, and the company sparkling. "

Maybe he was interested. Maybe he was going to ask her to marry him. Maybe there was hope of saving the farm yet.

Meg gave him her best coquettish smile and wink. "So are you going to give me the answer to my proposal or not?"

He placed his hat on his head and gazed at his horse as if he wanted to make a quick get away. "I like you, Meg. I like you a lot. But marriage is forever. I need more time before I can give you an answer."

Disappointment gripped her, and she couldn't restrain the frown she felt drawing her brows together. "I'm running out of time, Zach."

"What's the hurry?"

What did she say without telling him her reasons?

"I need your answer no later than next Saturday."

Zach opened his mouth to say something and then stopped. He nodded. "I'll let you know. Goodnight."

She watched as he rode off on his horse into the darkness. Why did everything have to be so hard? She understood his reasoning. She knew marriage was forever, but she was quickly running out of time. The bank loan would soon be due. She needed some quick cash.

Chapter Four

Meg opened the door and was greeted by her sisters with their arms crossed, their expressions a matching set of you-messed-up, waiting for her. Now she would have to face their wrath, and yet, she'd had no choice. She knew they were starving. They needed food.

"All right, I stole a ham. I was wrong," she admitted, throwing up her arms.

"And you kissed Zach. I saw you," Ruby said, her tone defiant. "I got into trouble for kissing boys."

"I'm older than you," Meg said defensively.

The memory of his kiss filled Meg with warmth in places she'd never before imagined. The sense that she was a woman, even though trousers covered her legs and a man's shirt habitually covered her breasts.

Annabelle's hazel eyes were cold, her expression stoic. "You might as well feed that ham to the chickens. We're not eating it."

"The chickens would be having a rich man's feast. Zach is going to pay Mr. Moore for his damn ham."

"Why did you do it, Meg? We're not starving," Ruby asked, staring at Meg like she didn't know her.

What could she say regarding her actions? No, she didn't believe in stealing, but they were trying so hard and getting nowhere. No matter how much she worked, it was never enough. "I'm sick to death of chicken. I can't bring myself to kill a goat, and the cows are for the market. Plus, I was starving."

She walked over to the table and began to clear the dishes. "I'm not throwing out this ham. You can now consider it a gift."

How embarrassing for the sheriff to know she'd stolen the ham and then to agree to pay for the meat to keep her out of trouble. It was generous, as he could have taken her to jail. What would her sisters have done then?

"Don't ever steal food for us again, Meg. You know Papa would not have agreed with what you did," Annabelle told her.

"Papa is not here to help us put food on the table." Weariness filled Meg's soul, leaving her bereft, empty. There was still mending for her to finish tonight. And Zach had not given her an answer. What would she do if he said no?

"Why didn't you just buy the ham?" Ruby asked.

"Because Ho Chinn hasn't paid me yet. Have either of you gotten paid?"

"No," Ruby said.

"I have some tips, though they're not much."

"Enough to buy a ham?" Meg asked, her voice rising with sarcasm as she clenched her fists. If only Ho Chinn would pay her what she was due.

"No."

"That's why I stole the ham," Meg said triumphantly as she finished clearing off the table and picked up more of her alterations. She worked day and night on these pieces of sewing, repairing, replacing broken buttons, and still, there was more work when she arrived at the laundry. More work and no pay.

Annabelle began to wash the dishes. "Papa always told us to stay on the right side of the law. Don't bring home any more stolen food."

Neither of them understood Meg considered herself a complete failure at taking care of them. She'd done everything she could and still it wasn't enough. "I know what Papa thought about stealing, but I couldn't watch the two of you getting skinnier and skinnier. It's my responsibility to make sure you're fed, and today I took matters into my own hands. I did what I had to do."

Ruby stared at her. "How is that any different from me earning money for Papa's birthday present? Stealing is stealing. Wrong is wrong. Don't do it again, Meg."

Meg sighed. How could she argue with her sisters when she knew they were right? Hopefully everything soon would be settled. She and Zach would be married, and he could help take care of her sisters. She sought to marry him for the right reasons, not just because he could help, but she was trying as hard as she could. She felt like she was running through water, getting nowhere fast.

And after that kiss this evening, maybe being married to Zach wouldn't be bad. She wouldn't mind spending time in his arms, his lips moving over hers. And the marriage bed...just the thought sent warmth spiraling through her body and giddiness filling her stomach. If kissing were that nice, what would marriage be like?

*

While Meg's body plowed the garden and took care of the necessary physical chores, her mind fantasized about the dress shop she'd own someday and the clothes she'd design. Doing the spring planting gave her plenty of time to dream. The ideas that flitted through her mind gave her hope and strength and helped her get the arduous chores done.

She would have a different future someday. Someday her dreams would be a reality. *Someday.*

The sun was sinking ever closer to the horizon, and her body ached from the day's labor. A cold wind blew from the north, a not-so-gentle reminder that winter was not finished.

She stopped, giving the horse a rest and her arms and her back a break. Almost done, she was ready to change out of these dirty clothes and spend the night working on the never-ending pile of mending.

She glanced off toward the south and saw a man riding in her direction. Squinting her eyes, she realized it was Deke. He'd come back, and her sisters would be falling all over each other in their haste to attach themselves to the handsome bounty hunter. She had to beat him to the house to stop the carnage and protect him from her wayward sisters.

Why was he returning so soon? Did he have news of Papa's killer? Anxious to learn the reason for his visit, she slapped the reins on the back of the horse, and the plow moved at a fast clip.

Quickly, she finished the last row and took the till and the horse to the barn. As she walked to the house, Deke rode into the yard.

Ruby threw open the door and danced out onto the porch. "Deke! You came back."

"Hello, Miss Ruby," he said, his voice a low, deep drawl as he tipped his hat. "Annabelle. Meg."

Throwing his leg over his horse, he slid to the ground. "How are you?"

Annabelle and Ruby were smiling at Deke like he

was Santa Claus in the flesh.

"We're great," Annabelle said, her voice a sultry mix of sweet Texas twang and southern comfort.

Ruby twisted her hands behind her back, pushing her breasts out toward the man. "Perfect as sweet peaches and cool lemonade."

Meg resisted the urge to give them both a good swift kick in the skirt. They couldn't have been more obvious with their eyes all dreamy, their voices dripping with honey, and their faces lit up like he was delivering presents. "Okay, ladies, why don't we invite the gentleman into the house."

"Come in, Deke. We were just about to sit down to supper," Ruby invited.

"There are still a couple of pieces of buttermilk pie left that I fixed for dinner last night," Annabelle promised, her smile gracing her face, her hazel eyes all warm and soft, like she would melt in a puddle at his feet.

"Thanks, ladies, I'm famished." He unstrapped his saddlebags, removed them from his horse, and carried them in his right hand.

Ruby stood back and waited for him to reach her side, where she promptly threaded her arm through his. He looked down at her, startled.

Oh, this was going to be an interesting night. One poor helpless man and two women chasing after him like they were cats in heat.

Annabelle opened the door and frowned at Ruby.

Meg followed them, shaking her head at her sisters' antics. This poor man had no chance around these women. It was a wonder they didn't smother him with their sultry looks and sweet as molasses voices.

"Did you catch James Rivera, the man who hurt our Papa?" Annabelle asked no sooner than the door closed behind him.

Deke smiled and sat his bags on the floor, letting his arm go limp. Ruby had to remove her hand. He opened the flap and pulled out several bundles of cash. Meg stared in disbelief as he raised and handed them to her.

"Your papa's part of the bounty. I caught the bastard down in San Antonio. After a brief struggle where he suffered a couple of black eyes and sore ribs, I turned him into the sheriff. " He smiled as he took off his dark cowboy hat and laid it on top of his things.

The girls squealed with delight.

"Oh, my gosh," Meg said, as she stared at the cash in her hands. It had to be several hundred dollars. Tears welled up in her eyes, closing her throat as her chest squeezed tightly. She refused to cry. She would not cry. She could not appear weak. Here was the bounty money her father lost his life over.

"Your papa was the one who convinced me to go after him and showed me how to find Rivera. Without his help, I would never have caught this bastard. You girls deserve his part." His warm emerald eyes pleaded with Meg to take the cash.

The cash felt dirty lying in her hand, and nausea clenched her gut. Blood money. Accepting part of the bounty was the last thing she wanted to do, but they were almost desperate. They were one week away from the bank taking the farm. "Deke, you deserve this cash. You caught that man."

"Take it, Meg," Annabelle beseeched. "That man is the reason our papa is dead."

Meg took a deep breath, knowing this would make

their lives so much easier. They needed this cash. This was what her papa was trying to earn to pay the note on the farm. She must accept the money; she had no choice. "Thank you, Deke."

Ruby threw her arms around Deke and pressed her young woman's body against him.

Annabelle moved toward Deke, but frowned as she watched her younger sister in his arms.

"Thank you, Deke," Ruby gushed. "Thank you for catching that man and helping us out."

Annabelle stepped back and stared at the bounty hunter.

When Ruby unfurled her young body from the man, Annabelle whispered, "Thank you. How can we ever repay you?"

He smiled at the group. "You can feed me. I'm starving."

For a moment, Meg thought she should warn Deke about her sisters, but then decided he was a grown man and he'd probably faced perils far more dangerous than two women. Ruby was vivacious, young, and flirtatious. Annabelle was just lonely and longed for a man of her own.

"Coming right up." Annabelle went into the kitchen where she started putting food on the table. "Ruby, can you help me please?"

Ruby sighed and went into the kitchen, leaving Meg alone with Deke. "Thank you, Deke. We were down to the blanket."

The money could help feed them and prepare for the spring planting season. It would do a lot for them, but it still seemed like blood money. The blood of her father.

His eyes widened in shock. "You were broke?"

"Yes, we were about to lose the farm. Papa went back to bounty hunting to make the balloon payment to the bank," Meg said, thinking what a generous man he was to bring back their papa's portion of the bounty. The very bounty that had killed him.

"Then I'm glad I could help," he said, his voice sincere, and she couldn't help but think if he married one of her sisters, he'd be a good man to have around.

"Dinner's ready," Annabelle called.

They all gathered around the table, and Deke took her papa's seat, where last night Zach had sat. Soon, she hoped Zach took her father's place in the family, but as her husband. They needed a man in their lives, and she wanted a husband. And Zach was a man whose kisses stirred her in ways she hadn't expected. In ways that left her reeling and wanting more.

Deke would be a worthy mate for one of her sisters, if he took the bait.

"Deke, let me fix your plate," Ruby said with a smile that could have charmed a snake.

Annabelle frowned at their younger sister and then held onto the ham plate until she could put the piece of ham on Deke's plate.

Oh my God, she was going to kill her sisters before this night was over!

Once they'd filled their plates, Meg asked the question that had been troubling her since Deke arrived. "How did you know where to find James Rivera?"

He smiled at them, his gaze blazed with warmth. "Your Papa told me wanted men at times return to where they're from. Usually wherever their families are, they would go back, even if they didn't stay long. If they had a wife and kids, they would want to see them and give

76

them money."

Meg listened with interest. That made perfect sense for a man to take his earnings and give them to his wife for her to use to buy food. Or even to return to his family to learn how everyone was doing.

"So Rivera went back to his family?" Annabelle asked.

Deke smiled at Annabelle and loaded his plate with the leftover ham and green beans. "He went back to his mother's farm. I'd heard his mother had taken ill, so I sat back and waited. I let him see her, but when he got ready to leave, I was waiting."

"Oh, I bet he was surprised to see you." Ruby gazed at him with awe and wonder in her big blue eyes.

"He'll be thinking about me for a long time in prison." Deke took a bite of the ham.

The girls weren't fussing about the ham now that Deke was here enjoying it. No one had refused to eat the meat tonight. But for now, Meg would no longer have to steal. They had cash; they could buy food.

Annabelle stared at him, her eyes all soft. "It's what he deserves. After all, he killed a bank teller, and our father lost his life chasing him."

"How many outlaws have you caught?" Ruby asked.

"About ten. But I don't plan on doing this forever. I'm hoping soon I can quit, buy me some land, and raise cattle." Deke smiled at the women, and Meg couldn't help but wonder if he was interested in either of the younger women.

Ruby flipped her long blonde curls over her shoulder and flashed her sapphire eyes and brilliant smile at him. "Maybe even get married."

She was wearing Meg's lipstick. Where had she

gotten the lipstick and where had she learned to be such a flirt?

He glanced over at her and smiled. "Maybe."

Good grief, if this was flirting, then no wonder Meg had never had a real man court her. She never would. It seemed silly to play the coquette. Why couldn't the man just accept her the way she was? Why did men want some silly flirtatious woman like Ruby?

"Why did you and Papa decide to go after Rivera? Why him and not some other criminal?" Annabelle asked.

Meg had to know the answer to this question, as well. What had been the decision making process when they'd decided on which outlaw to go after? Learning as much as possible about chasing criminals had suddenly become important.

"Your father insisted on not being too far away from you girls. So he always went after the men who were wanted in this area," Deke said.

"So how do you go about finding a man who's wanted by the law?" Meg asked.

He frowned and looked at her. "You find out where he was last seen or what his last job was and then if you can find out where his family lives, that's a good indication. You talk to people he talks to and then you go from there. If he's a bank robber, you look to see what banks he's hit and which ones he's missed. It's a grown up's version of hide and seek with guns."

Meg liked games. They were a challenge. And she liked to win. In fact, she insisted on winning.

Ruby pushed her plate away and leaned toward Deke, her chin resting on her palm, her eyes dreamy, and her bosom straining her dress. "Sounds so interesting."

Deke glanced around the table at the three of them, his eyes shifting nervously. "You're not thinking of doing some bounty hunting, are you?"

Meg looked at him shocked. "Of course not. We're women." Like that would stop her. Being a woman would probably help her catch the bastards.

Annabelle and Ruby laughed and shook their head.

"Oh, no," Ruby said, her painted lips in a perfect pout.

"We wouldn't know what to do with a criminal if we caught him," Annabelle exclaimed, pushing her chest out.

Good grief!

He laughed. "Yeah, that was kind of silly of me."

In that second, Meg's mind went a thousand different directions, but she refused to acknowledge the idea.

"We miss our papa, and when you talk about your life, it reminds us of him." Ruby turned her lips into a smirk as she looked at her sisters.

Meg knew that look, but she refused to recognize that Ruby was thinking in the same direction as Meg. She wasn't ready to face that knowledge just yet. She needed more time.

"Let me get you some pie," Annabelle said.

"Oh, I'll do it. You sit down, Annabelle." Ruby started to rise from the table.

If those two didn't fall to the ground and have a catfight over this man, it would be a miracle. "Why don't you both remain seated, and I'll bring the pie to the table." Meg stood, smiled at the women and Deke, and went to the kitchen.

Maybe they weren't looking at all their options. Maybe the three of them becoming bounty hunters was a way to keep from losing the farm. They had the necessary money to pay the loan, but what about next year?

Could they hunt men and turn them in to the law?

*

Dutifully, Ruby went to her job every day, though she secretly longed to do anything besides this boring scullery maid work. Even school had been more entertaining than scrubbing toilets and floors. What she really wanted was for her and Deke to run away, escape, and for the two of them to travel the world together. As she scrubbed the outhouse, she dreamed of how his body would feel laying naked against her own. Just the idea had her heart racing and her breathing quickening. God, she couldn't wait until they were man and wife.

Ruby finished cleaning the Mullen's outhouse and was now on her way back to the main house to do the dusting. So far today, she'd swept the floors, mopped the kitchen, and once she completed the dusting, she would find the head housekeeper and ask what else needed to be cleaned.

The work was not hard, just tiresome. Dealing with a cranky old housekeeper who came behind her and criticized everything she did was difficult. Okay, so maybe sometimes her work wasn't top notch, but if the housekeeper always found fault anyway, why try for perfection?

Opening the door, Ruby stepped into the hallway right into Clay Mullens, and his arms circled around her.

"Hello, beautiful." He pulled her up tight against him.

"Excuse me, sir, but this isn't appropriate." Fear strangled her like a gut line at a hanging, as he crushed her against his chest. Her lungs constricted making her breathing tight. She struggled against him.

"A girl who charges for kisses isn't exactly a proper young woman, is she?" he taunted, his voice deep and low against her ear. "I promise you, you'll enjoy this way more than you did those schoolboys in the play yard."

Dear God, how had he learned of her silly antic to raise money?

"That was a mistake," Ruby said, her voice suddenly shaky. She tried to put her arms between them, but he had them trapped down at her sides.

"Instead of paying you your housekeeping salary, what if I pay you to fuck me." He backed her up against the wall, pressing his erection between her legs.

She pushed him, but he was stronger than her, and he didn't budge. "Get off me! I'm not a calico queen you can use for your pleasure."

He reached up and grabbed her breast.

Revulsion swept through her, leaving her nauseous. "Stop! I told you no. I'm going to scream. Get off me."

"Relax, it will be fun. I'll make you feel good," he promised.

She opened her mouth to scream, and he covered her lips with his palm, silencing her. She yelled as loud as she could, and he slapped her. Stars appeared before her eyes and her cheek burned. She feared she would faint.

"I like a fighter," he whispered in her ear. "Do it again, so I can hit you again."

His hand over her mouth held her captive, fear clogged her throat like a man drowning in the river. She knew she was running out of time. Somehow she needed to outsmart him.

His lips kissed her neck, working their way down to her breasts. She tried again to push him away, but he was too strong, pinning her against the wall. The smell of him had nausea rising up in her throat. She couldn't breathe, she couldn't taste, but the sickening sour smell of him had her gagging. He sucked on her breasts through her clothing, gripping her hands in one of his large ones. He moved his body down hers and reached for her skirt.

She had to reach her gun before he discovered the holster beneath her skirt. Now she understood why her father had given them all shooting lessons and insisted they wear a gun at all times. Often she'd been tempted to leave the clumsy thing at home, but today she realized why he'd instructed them on how to take care of themselves.

The voice of the housekeeper and his mother coming toward them had him quickly pulling her into a closet and shutting the door. He leaned against the wall with her body pulled up against his own. In the darkness, he put his hand back over her mouth. "Shhh. Quiet. They'll soon leave, and then it will be just you and me, g'hal."

With one of his hands over her mouth and another on her wrists, she nodded her head, trying to make him think she was agreeing with him. He let go of her hand, and she tried to slip it beneath her skirt, but he grabbed her wrist again. Slowly, her eyes adjusted to the darkness and a sliver of light that came from a window above their heads.

"They're gone," he whispered. "Now for the fun."

No, no, no, they couldn't leave. They couldn't abandon her with him. She could feel her holster beneath her skirt, but she couldn't put her hand on the gun.

He placed her hand on his pants, and she could feel his rigid, hard member and fought against the urge to vomit. "Turn around and lift your skirt."

Ruby happily complied, reaching beneath her skirt and pulling her blue-lightnin' persuader out of its holster. Before he could undo his trousers, she whirled around to face him and cocked the trigger.

The sound had him backing away from her as he stared down at the pistol.

"Touch me again, and I'll put enough holes in you, they won't need to bury you." Ruby promised as she walked away from the wall, trying to reach the door.

He laughed. "Do I need to remind you that you need your job? Your father's dead. There's no one to defend you. You're a housekeeping whore."

When Clay walked toward her, she pointed the gun at him. "Stop!"

Revulsion swept through her, and she fought the urge to empty the chamber of the gun in his head. His family was wealthy, and the thought of swinging from a noose gave her itchy trigger finger pause. She had no one but her sisters. He had a wealthy family who could buy the law. Killing him was not an option.

"Put the gun away, you probably don't even know how to fire the thing." He laughed at her in the darkened closet.

Ruby's hand shook as she tried to rein in her anger, the need to kill him strong within her. Why tempt an armed woman with such a stupid comment? She raised the gun, took a deep breath, and steadied her arm. He needed to learn a lesson.

"Oh, yes, I do," she promised and pulled the trigger. The explosion in the closet almost deafened her as wood flew from the wall behind him. He screamed like she'd shot him, his face white, his eyes wide with fear, his hands shaking.

"You stupid bitch. The bullet went right by my ear."

"Consider yourself lucky. If I'd aimed for your head, you'd be dead right now."

His eyes were almost black as he stared at her, frightened. She didn't care. He looked at her like a man ready to run. He'd almost raped her, and she needed to inflict some of that same fear on him.

"I don't work for your family any longer. I don't need any job where I'm raped. Come toward me again, and the next bullet goes into your tallywhacker," she promised, more determined than she'd ever been in her fifteen years. No man was going to take what was hers to give and that included this lily livered skunk.

She walked backwards toward the door, the gun still in her hand. When she reached the doorknob, she twisted it and stepped right into the head housekeeper.

The woman stood there with her mouth open, staring at her. "You can't shoot a gun in the house. You're fired, Ruby."

"No, I quit." Ruby turned and walked out the back door of the house.

*

Ruby went to the livery stable and took the buggy and one of their horses, leaving the other horse behind for Annabelle. Right now, Ruby only desired to get home.

Shaking all over, she kept trying to wretch, but nothing came up. Tears flowed unheeded down her face. Her stomach roiled with fear, and she kept glancing back to make sure no one had followed her. She felt dirty. Soiled from his touch. He'd thought she would just willingly lie down on the floor and have sex with him. He thought wrong.

Clicking to the horse, she drove the buggy hard in her haste to get home where she would feel protected. Where she was safe.

If this was what lovemaking was all about, then she'd do without. She longed for a man to think she was beautiful and who spent time with her, kissing and getting to know her. And when the time was right, they would make love. Then afterwards she dreamed of him holding her in his arms and telling her how much he loved her.

The memory of Clay pinning her against his body, telling her of his plans to take her on the floor like she was a common whore, sent a shudder through her like the sound of a rattlesnake close by. Boys were so outrageous sometimes. They thought they were doing something so wicked when they'd kissed her out in the schoolyard, but she'd felt nothing. None of those boys meant anything to her. None of them. They were all silly boys who had no idea about the love of a good man and a woman. That's what she longed for, what she dreamed of.

A man like Deke.

She pulled the wagon into the yard of the house and saw Deke saddling his horse. He was a good man. A man worthy of her love.

"Deke, you haven't left yet," she called, pulling to a stop beside him. She tied the reins, and then Deke helped her out of the buggy.

The feel of his hands on her waist was warmer than the Texas sunshine and soothed her wounded pride. She longed for him to hold her and tell her everything would be okay.

"You've been crying," Deke said, gazing into her eyes. "What's wrong?"

She bit her lip to stop the trembling and then gasped. "I got fired."

"What happened?" he asked, his hands moving from her waist to her shoulder as he wrapped her into a hug.

Deke smelled of soap and something minty like he'd just bathed. The smell reminded her of the comfort of her father's bear hug. Deke's arms were strong and secure around her shoulders, and she leaned into him, needing his embrace. This man could be her husband, the one that understood her and made her feel special if she could convince him of how good they would be together. That she could make his life even better. That she would be a good wife. He would be hers.

"My sisters are going to be so mad at me. They're going to blame me, and it's not my fault." She sobbed into his shirt. "I didn't do anything wrong. Really, I didn't."

"I'm sure they'll understand."

"No, they're going to think that I...I instigated this, and I didn't. I promise you, I did nothing. Nothing."

Deke patted her shoulder as her tears increased, and she pressed her shivering body against him. The feel of Deke's muscled arms tightly wound around her was her undoing.

"He said...he said...I worked for his family, and to continue working for them, I'd have to have sex with him."

"Bastard," Deke swore.

"He was trying to force me," she wept.

"I'll kill him," Deke said, and her heart swelled, like a creek after a storm. Here was a man who was good and honest who would fight for her honor and protect her. Here was a man worthy of her love.

"He didn't..." Deke asked gently, wiping her tears from her face. His fingers were rough against her skin, but she didn't care.

"No, I pulled my gun on him. He backed off then, but the housekeeper was waiting for me when I came out of the closet, and she fired me."

Deke pulled her tight against him. "I'm sorry this happened to you. Men kind of lose their minds when a pretty girl like you is around them."

She looked up into his eyes. "Do you think I'm pretty?"

He swallowed. "Yes, I do."

The smell of leather and man swept over her. Here was a man who was kind and decent and all she'd dreamed of in a husband. Deke was a man who would love her and protect her and show her the meaning of life.

Living here, stuck on this farm with mere women, she longed to experience the life of adventure she dreamed of. One where she could kick the prairie dust off her feet and wear a party dress.

When her papa was alive, he'd been busy, though when he'd paid her attention, he called her his Ruby love. But since his death, there was no man in her life. No man to call her Ruby love. Only sisters who were going to be so angry with her when they learned she'd lost her job.

A shudder rippled through her, and she began to quake at the thought of what could have happened with Clay.

"Are you cold," Deke asked.

"No, just scared," she said. She bit her lip. "Please, Deke, wash away the memories of that awful man. Show me how a good man would treat a woman. Kiss me, make this fear go away."

He stared at her, his emerald eyes gazing at her, flickering with what looked like uncertainty. He opened his mouth, and she licked her lips.

"Oh, blazes," he said, as his mouth lowered to hers, and he covered her lips with his own. He tasted of apple, and a minty spice, and his lips plundered her. Ravaging her mouth, claiming her like she belonged to him. This was no schoolboy's blundering attempt, but a man who knew how to kiss her silly.

Only instead of satisfying her curiosity, she craved more. She needed more as she rubbed her fingers down the rock hard muscles in his back. A moan built in her throat as his tongue opened her mouth, and he pushed his way inside, causing her to gasp. She'd never experienced anything like this before, and the strength to resist seemed to leave her body. Her legs began to wobble, and his hands tilted her back, his arms holding her, supporting her as her breathing quickened, and she felt faint.

An ache began to build in the center of her body, and his hand slid across her breast. She didn't want him to ever cease. She needed him to touch her. To make her into a woman. A woman who knew how to please a man.

His lips left hers. "Stop."

Slowly, she opened her eyes to gaze up at him. Her body burned like a fire had been started, and she hungered to be consumed in its flames.

"No, don't quit. What you're doing is getting rid of the bad memories and feels so good," she gasped, still in his arms staring into his eyes. "You make me feel beautiful."

Not wanting this to end, she reached up, her fingers touching her lips and her body craving something she didn't understand. There was more, and she needed to experience it all. She needed Deke like she needed her next breath.

He raised her up until she was standing and then pushed her away from him, his strong arms out straight, putting distance between them. His breathing was quick and shallow, and his eyes were wild with an emotion she'd never seen before.

"No, I can't. That's as far as it goes. You're a child. You're innocent. And your papa would not have approved."

A child? He thought of her as a child? Did he not see the woman inside of her that was bursting for someone to release? Couldn't he see she was a woman fully grown?

"My papa is dead. We're alone, and I want to know what it feels like to be a woman. I want you to be the man who makes me into a woman." Ruby stepped toward him, needing him to take her into his arms once again.

"Oh, no, not going to happen with this man. I would be disrespecting your papa. I'm not having sex with a child."

"Stop calling me a child," she declared, her overwrought feelings rushing at her.

"That's what you are."

Like a splash of cold water had been thrown on her, shivers racked her body. She no longer had this intense urge for him to make her into a woman.

Tingles of rage crawled up her spine, and she went hot all over. First, she'd been almost raped, and now, the one man she desired was refusing her. She wanted to smash something, she wanted to hit him, she wanted to do something to make him hurt like she was hurting.

"Damn it, Deke Culver. I'm asking you to take me, and you're being all respectful. That's not what I want," she fairly screamed at him.

"It's not happening." He walked over to his horse where he finished tightening the cinch on his saddle. "Don't make me mad that I kissed you."

Tears pricked her eyelids as pain gripped her insides and twisted them into a knot. Her humiliation for the day was complete. Nothing worse could happen.

"Get off our land. Get out of here," she yelled, her rage full blown now that he was angry he'd kissed her. She reached beneath her skirt, giving him a flash of pantaloons and pulled her gun from its hidden holster.

With a toss of her blonde hair, she aimed the pistol at his groin. "Get the hell out of here."

He laughed at her. "Now you're proving to me you're still a child. You're not ready to be a woman."

She raised the gun and fired it over his head. "Get. Out. Of. Here. Now."

He climbed on his horse and then blew her a kiss. "See you round, Ruby. Save me a kiss when you're a grown woman."

"Aargh." She started to raise the gun again, but then remembered the words of her papa. *Don't aim a gun at a man unless you intend to kill him.* With a trembling hand, she lowered the weapon for the second time that day.

"You'll never get another one of my kisses," she yelled after him, but he only waved goodbye at her. The sun burned the tears tracking down her cheeks.

Men were ignorant beasts, and she wanted nothing more to do with them. She was done. She'd use them and

90

trample on their hearts and leave them behind in the dust
where they belonged.

Chapter Five

The restaurant had closed for the day, and Annabelle put the last of the clean dishes up in the cabinet. Then she took her apron off. "Anything else, Rusty?"

"Uh, I need to talk to you?" The tone of his voice was unsure, almost nervous.

Annabelle looked at him, and a nervous trickle ran down her spine. He had a sheepish expression on his face, not his regular leer, and he almost seemed embarrassed.

"I have to let you go."

"Why? I thought I was doing a good job?" Annabelle demanded, thinking of how hard she had worked to make sure she was doing everything right.

"You did." He looked at the floor and not at Annabelle. "It's just the wife caught me patting you on the ass the other day, and she said you have to go."

Anger stirred inside of Annabelle like a firestorm after a lightning strike. No, this wasn't her dream job, but it helped pay the bills. "Did you tell your wife I would serve you up to the buzzards if you touched me again?"

Her mother was probably rolling in her grave right now at Annabelle's language, but desperate times called for vulgarity. She was tired of being a proper lady and being taken advantage of.

"I did, but she didn't care." His eyes refused to meet hers, and she realized he wasn't as strong as he let on. His wife ruled the house and the business.

He rubbed his hand through his hair and then glanced at Annabelle. "She doesn't want any pretty young girl working here in the restaurant. She's going to take over being the waitress."

"Damn it, Rusty. I really needed this job. This work helps keep me and my sisters from starving." Annabelle wanted to hit the bastard. "You tell your wife you would have faced the barrel of my gun if you'd touched me again."

She was tempted to find his wife and let her know how foolish the woman was acting, not that she'd care. The woman feared Annabelle would take her precious man. Frankly, she wanted nothing more to do with this idiot.

Rusty stared as his mouth dropped open. She grabbed the money from his hand. It was hers. She'd worked hard and put up with bad customers, a touchy boss, and now his irate wife. She deserved more, but would take what she could get.

"It's three weeks salary. I gave you an extra week."

"Thanks," she said with a sigh, her heart heavy. What would she do now? "You're a bastard, Rusty. I worked hard for your restaurant."

He swallowed and gazed down at the floor. "I'd keep you, but the missus has not let me near her since she saw me touching you. I have to let you go."

The urge to take a frying pan and slap him upside the head was almost too much to bear. But she was never one for violence, and it wouldn't help the situation. Her best bet was to take her pride and go home. But damn, she hated losing this job.

"Next time, keep your hands to yourself."

He shrugged. "It's hard not to touch a pretty woman like you."

The audacity of the man. Maybe she'd be doing his wife a favor if she just pulled out a gun and shot him. But then the wife was the one insisting Annabelle leave, and frankly, neither one of these two fools was worth spending her life in prison. "Do you think I care?"

"No. You were a good waitress, Annabelle. If you need a reference, let me know, and I'll be happy to recommend you."

She stared at him unable to believe the nerve of this idiot. Had her father never let them work before because he knew what kind of people they would have to learn to deal with? Could he have known and not wanted his daughters subjected to morons who communicated with their hands.

The wife came to the door. "Rusty, it's time to go home."

He sighed, and Annabelle stood. "Thanks Annabelle. Good luck to you."

Annabelle stalked from the restaurant. She wanted to kill something. To take her gun and shoot at anything that moved at the moment.

Instead, she took the horse Ruby had left her and rode out of town. Damn, what would she tell her sisters?

*

It was quitting time. It was Friday. It should be payday. As Meg was leaving, she glanced over at her boss, half asleep in his chair. His wife was in the back, overseeing the laundry, while her husband took a nap.

94

The mending was finished, and Meg feared Ho Chinn wouldn't pay her for what she'd done. If he hadn't paid her a penny so far, who was there to require he compensate her for the work she'd done? What if he refused to give her the wages she'd earned?

"Ho Chinn," Meg called, waking him up from his slumber.

He glanced at her, his eyes drowsy. She almost hated this man. But yet, he had given her a job.

"When are you going to pay me?" she asked.

"Not today. Go home," he said.

"When are you going to pay me?" she asked again, her voice more demanding.

"Not today," he responded more adamantly and waved his hands at her. "Go home."

Fear trickled through her. Her fingers were sore; her eyes felt crossed, but the work was done. Completed. And now where was her compensation?

"Give me a date or I'm no longer working for you."

"I'm the boss. I will tell you when you get your money."

Fierce anger swept through her as she clenched her fists at his lack of feeling. Didn't he realize the reason she was working was because she needed money?

She stepped up to the counter and faced him, the cabinet separating them. "This is the last time I'm asking you, when will I see some cash from you?"

"I pay when you finish."

"I'm finished," she replied.

He glanced around at the stacks of mending. They were gone. Everything was done. She'd worked long and hard to clear up the stacks of repair work he had around the laundry.

Frustration gripped her insides, yet this was a job. She needed it so she could make next year's bank payment. She needed it to help feed her sisters. She needed this job so she could develop a reputation as a good seamstress.

"Go home, come back tomorrow."

"I've been working for you for two weeks. I did all the mending; now it's time for you to give me my wages."

He glanced around the laundry in disbelief. "Everything done?"

"Yes, everything's done."

"Go home, come back tomorrow."

"Pay me now!" she demanded.

"No," he said. "More work tomorrow."

A fierce burning sensation fired through her at the injustice of everything in the last few weeks. Her father's death, the bank note, and working so hard to take care of things and being thwarted at every move she made. Jumping over the counter, she watched as his eyes grew large, and he stood.

"What are you doing? Go home now!"

"I'm collecting my wages." She opened up the cash register. "I finished. You need to pay me."

For two weeks, she'd worked twelve to sixteen hours a day to complete the mending so the money she earned could help at home, but now she wasn't even sure he would ever give her the cash due her. It was time to collect.

He came up behind her and grabbed her hand to keep it from getting inside his cash drawer. "Go home. No pay today."

She grabbed him by the collar of his shirt and pushed

him to the laundry rack where there was a hook on a pulley that lifted the laundry basket. The laundry maids would pull the baskets into the back where they proceeded to wash the clothes.

"Stop," he yelped.

She'd put up with him for over two weeks, checking each piece, making sure she had done it perfectly, bringing some back and saying redo, carrying mending home, and working late at night to get his laundry caught up for naught.

Holding him by the shirt, she put his vest through the hook, lifted him off the ground and then pushed him toward the back, sending him zipping into the back along the wire.

He screamed in his native tongue at her. Finally, his English kicked in. "You fired. Do not come back. You fired."

Meg opened the cash register and counted out what was owed her and left the rest. It was tempting to take what wasn't hers, but that wasn't money she'd earned. She only took her wages and then slammed the drawer shut.

"Goodbye, if you ever need another seamstress don't call me." She walked out the door.

The money she'd earned was less than sixty dollars. Not enough to pay off the loan completely. If they paid off the bank loan in full, there would be no pressure to save the farm. There would be no pressure to take jobs that were demeaning and paid less than a crib girl's salary.

*

Ruby heard the gunshots and rushed outside to see who was shooting. Annabelle had set up the tin cans on the fence where Papa had taught them to shoot. One by one she knocked off the cans.

"Hey," Ruby called.

"Hi," Annabelle fairly grunted.

"You okay?" Ruby asked, noting the rigid set of Annabelle's shoulders and the tense lines around her mouth.

Annabelle raised her pistol; her eyes focused on the target and then pulled the trigger, knocking the can to the ground. "See the face on that can?"

"You drew a face on a can?"

"Yes," Annabelle raised her pistol, sighted her target and fired at the can. It flew off the fence and landed with a bounce on the ground. "I'm killing my boss."

Ruby gave a little laugh. "You're speaking figuratively, right?"

Not sensible, logical, and rational Annabelle. Of the three, she was the least likely to commit bloodshed. What had happened to make her want to kill her boss?

"Maybe, I haven't decided yet." Annabelle looked fierce, madder than Ruby had ever seen her. "I'm going to put a bullet through his forehead." She fired her Baby Dragoon Colt. "Bull's eye."

Ruby laughed, lifted her skirt and pulled out her own gun. "Let me have a try. That can is Clay Mullens."

Taking aim, she pulled the trigger and knocked the can off the fence. There was satisfaction in pretending she'd just shot a man who'd tried to rape her. The law would never do anything to stop him, and she feared his family would somehow retaliate if she were to have him arrested. It would be her word against his, and he would win.

"Knocked his head clean off? Now I think I'll aim for

his man parts." She fired again, and the next can flew off the fence and rolled along the ground, making a clattering noise.

Annabelle turned and stared at Ruby a moment, her gaze suddenly suspicious. "Why are you aiming for his man parts?"

Ruby lifted her arm, gripped the handle with both hands and sighted the target. Pulling the trigger, she released the tension that had gripped her all day. "The asshole tried to rape me today. I wanted to kill him. I raised my gun and was ready to put one in his head, but I knew I'd go to jail. I fired close enough he heard the bullet whiz by. I think he might have messed his pants. Then I quit."

Tears of anger and fear at the experience bubbled up inside, overwhelming her as she realized what would have happened if she'd had no gun. "I'm sorry. I worked hard; I did what I was told, but I wasn't going to have sex with him. I just wasn't."

Now, she would hear the lecture on how it was time to grow up and think of the three of them. Now, Annabelle would make her feel like a complete failure, but it wasn't her fault. Not this time.

Annabelle laid her gun down on the fence and walked over to Ruby and hugged her close. "It's okay. I'm so glad he didn't hurt you. You know Meg would have killed him if he had."

Ruby held onto her sister, her body shaking with the realization of how close she'd come to being raped. "I was so scared, Annabelle. My cheek is sore from where he hit me. Other than that, I'm okay."

"You're not going back there," Annabelle said, her hand gently touching Ruby's bruised cheek.

"No, I was fired."

Annabelle laughed and stepped out of her sister's embrace. "I was let go today as well."

"What?" Ruby stared at her sister in surprise. Annabelle had been fired, as well?

"Yeah, Rusty's wife caught him grabbing my ass and told him he had to let me go."

"He touched you inappropriately?"

"Yes," Annabelle said quietly. "I did nothing to provoke him."

"Me neither," Ruby responded, thinking of how she'd only spoken to that creep once. Just once.

Annabelle had dealt with an unwanted man touching her, and Ruby had a young man who tried to rape her. Poor Meg was continually working, doing the mending, and hoping Ho Chinn would pay her. They all had horrible jobs, except that Annabelle and Ruby were now fired.

Annabelle picked up her gun, took aim, and fired at another tin can. "But he promised me he'd give me a good recommendation."

"You or your ass?" Ruby laughed and wiped away her tears. She loved Annabelle and now realized how she had let Deke Culver, the sorry maverick, come between them. Never again.

Annabelle smiled. "Probably my ass."

Ruby picked up her gun and fired at the last tin can, knocking it down. Annabelle hurried over and set them all up on the fence again. "Okay, so let's tell our bosses how we really feel about them and then shoot the can that represents their sorry, butts. You go first."

"Touch me again, and I won't hesitate to put a bullet through your brain." Ruby fired the gun, sending the can flying through the air before it landed on the ground.

The image of his face swam before her and a rush of pleasure erupted inside her at the idea of target practicing with his face.

Annabelle lifted the revolver and aimed. "Put your hands on your wife's butt, not mine."

"I'm not a calico queen," Ruby spat and then knocked the can to the ground.

"Tell your wife she's one unlucky woman to be married to scum like you." Annabelle took aim on the can and fired.

What had Annabelle put up with before his wife caught the jerk? Why hadn't she told them?

Ruby aimed her small Baby Dragoon Colt. "Just because I work for your family, doesn't mean I'm your personal whore."

Annabelle steadied her pistol and aimed it at the can. "No, I don't want to become a painted cat."

A painted cat? A saloon girl? Where had that come from? Surely Annabelle didn't think they would be so desperate they'd have to work in a saloon. No, Ruby wasn't ready for that job, and she'd do everything she could to keep from having to sell herself. Today had shown her she didn't want anything to do with men.

"All men are outlaws, even you, Deke Culver," Ruby said, firing the gun.

Annabelle frowned and glanced over at Ruby. "You're not in love with him any longer? When did that change?"

Oops! She shouldn't have mentioned Deke's name. Yet anger rose up in her and gripped her hand, pulling her trigger finger. The tin receptacle flew off the fence, clattering when the bullet hit the metal.

"I was in infatuation, not love. But all that changed this afternoon when I came home. I don't think he'll be back anytime soon." Ruby raised her gun. "We both dodged a bullet with that one."

"How do you know?" Annabelle asked, staring at Ruby with those all-knowing eyes that always found out whenever Ruby did anything wrong.

"He told me I was a child. He wouldn't…"

Annabelle started to laugh. "So he is a good man and wouldn't take advantage of you. You need to leave him to a woman."

"Oh yeah, you want him, and I should leave him for you. Well, let me tell you, I don't think he'll be coming around again, after I fired my gun at him."

Twice today she'd aimed her gun, at a man close enough to send a message. A leave me alone message. Still, Deke was no different from any other man she'd ever met.

"Ruby?" Annabelle said. "You fired at our guest."

"Yes, after he kissed me and then wouldn't continue."

Oh, she probably shouldn't have told her sister that little piece of information. But it was true. Why wouldn't he continue kissing her? Didn't he enjoy kissing her? Why had he stopped?

Ruby took aim with her pistol and fired at a canister. "That's for you, Deke."

"You know, I never was really attracted to him. But I would like to have a man in my life. Someone who cared for me. Someone I could make a life with," Annabelle said gazing off in the distance.

Stunned, Ruby looked at her sister in surprise. She didn't want him for herself? Then suddenly it dawned on her. "You were trying to keep me from him."

"I don't think you're ready for a man," Annabelle said softly. "But maybe I was wrong. You're growing up, and we've all been through so much. Maybe I should just stay out of your way."

Ruby smiled. "Thank you, but Deke is not who we thought he was. He's not a man who…" she trailed off. So he wouldn't bed her. Didn't she want a man who respected her? Or did she just want a man she could manipulate?

For a moment, Ruby considered her thoughts, leaving her all tied up. Finally, she raised her gun, aimed, and fired at a can on the fence.

"What in the hell is going on here?" Meg called out, standing behind Ruby and Annabelle.

They both whirled around, startled at the sound of her voice. "It sounds like you guys have started a war."

"We just may," Annabelle said. "I was 'let go' today."

"I quit."

Meg started to laugh, her voice sounding hysterical.

Ruby laid her gun down and went to her older sister's side. She'd never seen Meg so vulnerable. So on the edge that she worried her. She laid her hand on Meg's arm. "Are you okay?"

"What's so funny?" Annabelle asked, gazing at Meg like she'd lost her mind.

"I got fired today too," she managed to get out from between her hysterical laughs.

For a moment, Ruby's stomach sank, and she felt nauseous and light-headed. They had no money coming in. None. What would they do?

Annabelle took a deep breath and handed her the gun.

"There's one can left. It's your turn."

Meg dried her eyes and glanced at the gun she held in her hands, and then she looked out at the tin left on the fence. She raised the pistol and just as she pulled the trigger said, "Die you bastard, die."

The can clinked against the ground as it rolled.

"Should I set them up again?" Ruby asked, wondering if Meg needed to do more shooting to let off some steam.

"No, we need to save our bullets," Meg said with a sigh. "But thanks for helping me let off some frustration. He wasn't going to pay me."

"The son tried to rape me."

"Ruby, are you all right?" Meg asked, touching Ruby on the arm. "He didn't harm you?"

They weren't mad at her, and that made all the difference in the world. Ruby had never tried to make this boy like or want her. She'd done nothing, and he'd taken advantage of her. "I'm okay. I did what Papa taught us; I pulled my gun on him."

"Rusty's wife caught him grabbing my ass. She doesn't want me around anymore," Annabelle said, taking aim with her pistol.

"You continued to work there after he'd grabbed you on the ass? Do I need to go take care of him?" Meg asked.

"No, I think his wife beat him up pretty good. I hated that job."

Ruby stared at her sisters, and a fierce feeling of love and affection consumed her, overflowing her heart and filling her eyes with tears. They were all she had. They were the two people on this earth who cared what happened to her, and she would do whatever was necessary to help protect them. No matter what else happened, she could always count on them.

"What about you? How did you get fired?"

Meg bit her lip. "I finished the mending and still he wouldn't say when I'd receive my pay. I don't know if he ever would have paid me, so I took what was mine."

Annabelle laughed. "You took money from the cash register, didn't you?"

"I only took what was owed me."

Ruby shook her head, staring in wonder at them, yet she also had such fierce love for her sisters. "What are we becoming?"

Meg glanced at her and sighed. "I don't know. What are we going to do now?"

"I refuse to work as a maid again." Never again would Ruby be on her hands and knees in someone else's kitchen while their son lingered in the shadows waiting for her. Never.

Annabelle shivered. "I'm not going to be a waitress again."

Meg didn't say anything. "Let's go eat dinner. We'll worry about this tomorrow."

"There's still Zach." Ruby said.

She wondered if Meg wanted to marry the good-looking sheriff. He wasn't bad on the eyes, and she'd appeared to enjoy kissing him the other night when they'd peeked out the window at them.

"The deadline is tomorrow," Meg said.

***

Meg went to the bank and paid the balloon payment. The expression on the banker's face as she counted out the bills and asked for a receipt was one she would treasure. The old buzzard had been expecting to repossess and instead she'd paid him for the year.

They had one year to collect enough money for the next balloon payment. One year, no jobs, and no income. She didn't have to marry Zach, she had some time now, but part of her didn't want to let him go. She *wanted* to marry Zach.

Annabelle and Ruby were at the general store buying supplies and stocking up on food items. They would have enough to get them through the summer, and then they had twelve months to earn the money for the next balloon payment. Twelve months.

They were three women in a small town, in desperate need of a way to make a living.

Meg had to know Zach's decision. She had to know if he would marry her and become a partner on the farm.

Walking down the wooden sidewalk, her boots made a clunking noise as she strode towards Zach. Outside the sheriff's office, she noticed the wanted posters up on the wall. Wanted for stealing—fifty dollar reward. Wanted for murder—five hundred dollar reward. Wanted for robbery—two hundred dollar reward. No wonder Papa had been a bounty hunter.

She opened the door and walked into the sheriff's. One of the deputies sat behind the desk. He glanced up at her and smiled a knowing smirk that left her uneasy.

"Where's Sheriff Zach?"

"He's down at the bath house. Don't know why he likes to bathe so often. Heard he planned on doing some courtin' tonight. Heard your name mentioned. Also heard him mention the saloon."

Meg frowned. He mentioned the saloon? If he were going to marry her, he wouldn't be going to the saloon.

"Thanks, tell him I came by," she said and walked

out the door.

He was at the bathhouse. Maybe she should go back to the house and just wait for him, or find someplace and sit and rest a spell while he finished. No, she needed an answer. She needed one now. No decisions about what to do could be made until after she'd talked to Zach.

The sun was dipping below the horizon; the small town was shutting down, and the saloons were beginning to wake from their day of slumber. Meg wanted to get home before the rowdies came out to play.

Annabelle and Ruby drove up in the buggy and pulled alongside her as she sat on her horse.

"Did you talk to Zach," Ruby asked.

"No, I haven't found him yet." Never would she mention to her sisters that he was at the bathhouse, and she intended to go find him. They would never understand her need to know his answer now.

Annabelle gazed at Meg a frown on her face. "Are you okay?"

"I'm fine. Nervous, but fine."

"We're going home so we can get everything unloaded and put away before dark," Annabelle said, nodding her head.

"Okay, I'll meet you at the farm."

"Good luck. See you at home," Ruby called as Annabelle clicked the reins of the horse, and the buggy pulled away.

What should she do? Wait here in the street for Zach or go to the bathhouse? She was tired; she was ready to go home, and she needed her answer now.

With a flick of the reins, her horse trotted down the street to the bathhouse. When she arrived at the establishment, she swung her leg over her horse and dropped to the ground. She tied the reins to the hitching post and took a deep steadying breath. Going into the all-male establishment would not be easy.

By now the street was cloaked in a dusty shade of orange as the last rays of the sun shone before it sank beneath the horizon. Good, decent folks were starting to go inside, and soon the street would be filled with music from the saloons. Men would be carousing the streets, drinking and gambling. She would talk to Zach and then get home.

Meg walked to the door and went inside. A man met her at the door. "We don't allow women."

"I know," she said impatiently. "I'm looking for the sheriff."

"He's in the back and you can't go in there."

"The hell I can't." She began to walk to the area he'd pointed to.

After only a few steps, she heard the laughter.

"Those pants she wears fit her real nice."

"Yeah, her ass looks sweet and tempting."

"I don't want any sage hen who can out shoot me and doesn't dress like a woman."

Heat flooded her face as embarrassment gripped her. She felt like her chest was ripped open, leaving her vulnerable. They were serving her up, talking about her. They were making fun of her because she dressed like a man. Pain spiraled through her; tears welled up and threatened to spill. How could they be so unfair?

She wanted to wear a dress, she wanted to look and act like a woman. She dreamed of owning a dress shop, but right now she had no choice in her outfits. She didn't even own a dress that fit her any longer. She'd given her last dress to her sisters and taken to wearing Papa's pants. She longed to design a pattern and stitch a dress, but there was no money for the cloth.

"Yeah, but whoever she marries, who's going to be wearing the pants in the family?"

"You could be one of those hen-pecked husbands. 'Yes, dear, whatever you say, dear,'" a man said in his imitation of a woman's voice.

A new round of laughter accompanied this statement and tears pricked Meg's eyes and filled her throat. She would not cry.

"In bed, I bet she's colder than a well digger's ass in Montana. She'd probably want to take the lead. 'Roll over honey, I'm doing the pushin'.'"

"Gentleman, the lady looks awfully fine in her britches. If that's the worst thing her husband has to endure, then I don't think the job would be that bad. But sometimes her nature is a little bossy. She likes to take control," Zach's voice called out. "But in my marriage, I wear the pants, I make the decisions, and I take the lead in the bedroom."

"Not with that biddy you wouldn't."

She held her breath, waiting for him to fight for her, to tell these men that she was a good woman who'd been dealt a difficult situation and done the best she could. She kept waiting for him to list her good qualities. She kept waiting and realized he wasn't going to defend her. The no-good bastard was just going to let these men ridicule her.

She was bossy? She liked control? What did he expect? When she'd taken over the responsibility of her family, she'd had to change from a child to a woman. Something a twelve-year-old young'un should never have to do. She'd had no choice.

Meg's insides tightened, and a rush of fury consumed her, leaving her hair ends almost standing on end. The urge to storm in there and tell everyone he was the biggest damn fool that ever lived had her feet moving, but then she stopped. No...wait.

Running in there like a frenzied angry woman would complete her humiliation. They would love to see her breakdown in a fit of anger. The whole town would hear of how she'd been stripped of her pride in the bathhouse. There were other ways to extract her revenge.

She turned and faced the man running to stop her. "I'm sorry, I don't know what I was thinking. I can't go back there. I'll just wait outside for him."

He wiped his forehead with a handkerchief. "Thank you. I didn't want to have to carry you out."

A snide laugh escaped her lips. "That wouldn't have happened."

Opening the door, she walked out and untied the reins of her horse and rode around to the back of the bathhouse where the private tubs were kept. Most men had a drink while they waited for their bath to be prepared and then went to the private areas to soak. She'd be waiting.

Tying the reins of her horse, she peered beneath the tented area. The man who owned the bathhouse had yet to build a permanent establishment. Laid out on her belly, she crawled under the canvas and spied the big round tin tubs. Yeap, they'd do.

After returning to her horse, she searched and found the coil of rope in her saddlebags. With a loop and a knot, she tied the rope to her saddle horn and then strung it through her stirrups. She found the smaller thinner rope she kept just for hog tying, grabbed a rag and stuffed them in her pocket. At the edge of the tent, she waited on her belly for Zach, hoping she'd chosen the right room.

A man came in and poured two buckets of hot water into the tub and then a smaller bucket of cool water. "It's ready for you, sheriff."

He walked into the area; a towel draped around his waist.

"Thanks, I'm going to rest a bit. If I'm not out in thirty minutes, come wake me," he instructed the man. "I've got plans tonight, and I need to be out of here in less than an hour."

"Will do, sir," he acknowledged.

Meg smiled. He'd be awake in thirty minutes. As he dropped the towel, she gazed in interest. Not bad. Not bad at all. Her stomach tightened, and her breathing quickened. A nicely built man with a muscled chest, tight stomach, and strong thighs. Too bad the cowboy would never get the opportunity to show her his physique in a marriage bed.

Zach turned his back, his buttocks a nice firm shape she longed to slap. He sunk down low into the tub. He was too big to sprawl out, but he placed his towel beneath his head and scooted down into the water. He sighed a contented, relaxed sound. Though she was unable to see his eyes, she'd just bet they were closed.

She loosened the strings on the tie downs on the tent, not wanting to tear up the man's place of business, and then waited.

About ten minutes later, the sheriff's breathing evened out, and she knew he was sleeping. She took out her tools, crawled on her belly into the tent and then came up behind him. With her lasso ready, she jerked his feet up and slipped the rope around his ankles, tightening the slipknot. His eyes flew open in surprise as she wrapped the other end of the rope around his wrists, effectively hog-tying the bastard.

"What are you doing in here?" he yelled, trying to rise, his brown eyes stunned and questioning. "You tied me up? What are you doing?"

"Did you tell anyone I'd asked you to marry me?" she asked.

"No," he stammered and she knew he lied. "I planned on coming out to your place tonight to ask you to marry me."

Yeah, and her chickens were going to lay golden eggs.

She wrapped the rope around the tub and tied it. "Marry a woman wearing pants? Sure, you were going to ask this *bossy, controlling* woman to marry you. You *like* being hen-pecked."

"How did you hear?" His eyes widened in disbelief, his forehead drawing together creating a wrinkle above his brows, as he realized she'd heard everything.

She paused and smiled down at him, then leaned into the tub.

"Let's just say the walls have ears." The shock and surprise on his face was almost gratifying. What if she hadn't come in here late this afternoon? She would never have known his true feelings.

"What are you doing?" he asked, seeming to just notice she continued to wrap the rope across the top of the tub.

"I'm securing you in. Don't want you to catch cold," she replied in that happy singsong voice she used when she was so angry she had to cover her tone. "Someone might see your…" She gazed down into the tub, and he pulled his legs together as best he could. "Private parts."

"God damn it, Meg."

Her chest tightened, and her eyes watered. She shoved the pain of his rejection deep inside, now was not the time to let him see how much he'd hurt her. Now was the time to get her revenge, but why didn't it feel better? Why wasn't she enjoying making him suffer? Why did it hurt so much?

"You don't want a woman wearing pants."

"I didn't say that. I can't help if it they were making fun of you, I was trying to defend you."

"Oh yeah, and you were doing such an outstanding job." Peering into his face, she pretended to study him. "Why, I can see the hen pecks from here, you big sissy," she said, tying the last knot. "Yes, I'm so sure you wanted 'the job.'"

"I want to marry you," he said, almost screaming at her.

"And I want a man who will defend me, stand up for me, and tell bastards like that to shut the fuck up about my wife. Do you understand? I don't want a scalawag, lowlife jackeroo for a husband." Before he could respond, she shoved the rag into his mouth.

Now she'd no longer have to listen to his empty promises of how he wanted her to marry him. Now, her eyes wouldn't be tearing up at his assurances of wedding bliss.

His eyes grew large, and he struggled against the ropes.

"That's better. I won't have to listen to your bullshit." She checked her knots one more time.

"This won't take long, but I wouldn't move around too much. I'd hate to tear the bottom out of that tub and have your bare ass be dragged along the street. That might hurt a bit," she said and tied the tent flap up. With a swing of her leg, she climbed onto her horse and gigged him with her heels.

The horse grunted, but slowly the tub began to move as she dragged it over rocks and grass as it moved out of the tent.

Zach was screaming at her through the gag, making, gargled noises, but she ignored him as her horse tugged the tub from the alley, turning and heading toward Main Street. Slow and steady she went, not wanting to hurt Zach, just humiliate him. The way she'd been demeaned in public.

She pulled the reins to a stop about a block from the saloon, between the bank and the mercantile. From here, she could hear the piano music tinkling, the loud laughter and the singing, but there was very little foot traffic.

It would be a while before Zach was found, though she knew he'd be located before daylight and the night was warm enough he wouldn't be in any danger. Only the danger of shame and mortification and she'd suffered that plenty.

For a moment, her conscience pricked. He'd said he was going to ask her to marry him. Maybe she was acting in haste. Maybe she should have given him a chance to explain. But maybe the bastard was just like every other man in this town and thought less of her because she wore pants.

"This is the end of the road, fiancé," she said sarcastically, trying to cover the pain. "I'm sure you'll soon be found, but your pride might be a little dinged. Tied up, unshucked, and wet in the middle of Main Street. Kind of like how I feel when men say ugly things about these pants I wear. Or they say her ass looks really nice in those trousers. 'I don't want a woman who can out shoot, out rope, or out smart me.' If you wanted a stupid, simple-minded dress-wearing woman, then we were never meant to be together."

Untying the rope from her horse, her heart in her throat, she called, "Goodbye, sheriff."

Zach started banging against the tub, but Meg spurred the horse and rode away.

As she left, her heart squeezed painfully, and tears blurred her vision. She would not cry. She would not cry. Any man who didn't love her for who she was and accept her the way she was didn't deserve her.

Life had made her tough. Life continued to show her she couldn't be meek or mild or weak. Meg had to be strong for her sisters. And now she knew the answer to her decision.

*

Meg walked into the house. Annabelle and Ruby sat at the table. They glanced up at her, and she shook her head. The words refused to come out; her pride still smarted, and her heart felt beaten up.

"Bastard," Ruby said.

"Scalawag. Are there no good men left?" Annabelle asked.

"I don't think we'll be seeing any more of Zach," Meg replied, her heart shattering in a thousand pieces inside her chest. After what she'd done to him, he would never forgive her and yet he'd hurt her, as well.

"What happened?" Annabelle asked.

"Let's just say he's too tied up at the moment to marry me."

"Meg McKenzie, what in the hell did you do?" Ruby

asked, her blue eyes shining with laughter. "And everyone wonders where I get my wild side."

Meg didn't feel good about leaving Zach naked on Main Street and had even considered returning and untying him, but she feared the consequences.

"I overhead Zach making fun of me wearing pants with the other men in town," the admission was humiliating, and Meg's chest ached from the need to cry, but she refused. She would not cry.

Her sisters rose and came over to her. They each hugged her. "I'm so sorry."

Meg had to fight to keep tears from falling.

Ruby held on to her, clasping her against her small frame. "You're beautiful, Meg, and any man who can't see that shouldn't be with my sister."

"He doesn't know what he's missing." Annabelle took a step back from her sister. "He didn't deserve you."

"Thanks, but there's nothing like overhearing a bunch of men talking about how your ass fits nicely in a pair of trousers." Meg shook her head. With a sigh, she sat down at the table and the others followed.

They were back to square one. This time they had twelve months to earn enough money to save the farm. But how would they make that next balloon payment?

"What are we going to do now?" Ruby asked.

Meg rubbed her hand across her face, her heart wishing so badly for Papa. She longed for his guidance. "I paid the loan on the farm, so we're good for now, but that's not going to keep us fed. Next year we'll have the same problem."

Annabelle smiled that knowing way of hers Meg knew meant she had an idea. "I think I have a solution." Jumping up from the table, she went into her room. A few minutes later, she returned with a stack of wanted posters and laid them on the table. "I think we have to do what Papa did. I think we have to become bounty hunters."

"But we're women," Ruby said, glancing down at the men. "These guys aren't exactly attending church every Sunday. How will we find them?"

"We do what Deke said he and Papa did. We learn where they're from. Where their family lives. We search them out. Just one of these will pay more than what we earned at our fine jobs that got us nowhere," Annabelle said.

"We could get hurt. Papa died chasing a criminal. We could be shot or captured or even worse," Meg said. "We could die."

"We could die plowing," Ruby said.

"Or we could pay off the farm," Annabelle said softly. "Never have to worry about losing it again."

Ruby's eyes widened, and her face glowed with excitement. "And think of the adventures we'll have. Trapping outlaws and turning them in to the sheriff."

"They're not going to go willingly," Meg reminded Ruby.

Ruby smiled, her blue eyes dancing with excitement. "No, but I think we're strong women who can hold our own against any man."

"We can outshoot most men," Meg said, thinking of what the town men had said about her today in the bathhouse. "Even if we just go for the sly dogs, we could earn a better living than what we've been doing." Who was she kidding? She'd been thinking about this for weeks. She'd been considering and reconsidering if this was a viable option for them to chew over. But did she want to risk her sister's lives?

"Once we paid off the bank note, all we'd have to do is raise enough cattle to keep us fed," Annabelle, the logical one of the three said softly.

An uneasy silence fell between the women.

"What about our stock? The garden?" Meg's main concern was the farm. After everything they'd gone through, she wasn't ready to lose their farm. "Who's going to take care of the farm?"

"Either one of us stays here alone, or we sell the livestock, or we hire someone to look after them while we're gone," Annabelle said. "I could stay here or we can hire someone. But we must never hunt alone. We're a team. We do this together."

Meg contemplated her options. This very thought had swirled around in her mind for days. Their father had made a decent living as a bounty hunter. Why couldn't they? Why couldn't they catch criminals and turn them in?

Why couldn't they pay off the mortgage and put some money in savings and then come back with the dream of farming full time? Maybe they'd find husbands or men they liked while doing this, and maybe they'd get injured and have to quit or maybe they'd make more money than they dreamed of because men were blind to a pretty girl. While Ruby flirted, Meg would be slapping the cuffs on them.

"I'm in," Meg said.

"I'm in," Ruby said.

"I'm in," Annabelle replied. "And here is our first job."

Meg got up and poured them each a small sip of the whiskey her father had kept on hand for special occasions. She gave each woman a glass. They raised it up. "To new beginnings where the men are dangerous, the trail is dusty, and the women are deserving. To the bounty hunter sisters—Lipstick and Lead."

Dear Reader,

Thank you for reading *Desperate.* I hope you enjoyed the lead off story for my brand new western historical romance series, *Lipstick and Lead.* The next three books are each sister's story, starting with Meg. *Deadly* will be out the end of July.

Lend it. Please share this book with a friend.

Recommend it. Nothing makes a writer feel better than when you recommend their work to other readers. If you enjoyed the book, please tell your friends.

Review it. Authors really appreciate it when you leave a review on Goodreads and the vendor you purchased it from. Reviews from readers have the power to make or break a book. Whether positive or negative, thank you for taking the time to review my story. I'd be lying if I didn't say I go out and take a look at the reviews.

If you'd like to know when a new book is coming out, win free books, or just know what's going on with Sylvia, please sign up for my newsletter at www.sylviamcdaniel.com

.

Thanks so much for reading *Desperate.* For a list of my other romances and a sneak preview of *Deadly*, please turn the page!

Yours in Drama, Divas, Bad Boys and Romance

Sylvia McDaniel

Deadly

Chapter One

Meg McKenzie stood in yet another hotel room, in another dusty frontier town, on the hunt for yet another wayward criminal. She pulled her Baby Dragoon revolver from her holster, spun the cylinder, and checked to make sure a bullet graced every chamber. With a gentle tug she checked the leather case, and then slid the weapon back into the holster, just a fingertip away.

"The McKenzie sisters are about to strike again," her sister Ruby said, as she slid her own gun into the hidden sheath-like case neatly tucked beneath her petticoats. Her saloon dress dipped low in the front to the edge of her breasts, the straps completely off her shoulder. She flipped her blonde hair back and checked her image one last time in the mirror. "How many men have we brought to justice?"

"At least twelve. Seems we've spent more time on the road than we have at home," Meg said, homesickness surging through her like an open wound.

In the last year, they had learned the bounty hunter trade and continued their father's legacy. With his death, the girls had been forced to find work in order to save the farm and in a desperate moment had chosen their current path. Meg and Ruby chased wanted criminals, whereas Annabelle ran the business side of their bounty hunting and maintained their family farm. At least until they returned and could join their sister once again. They never intended to make this their lifelong occupation. Just long enough to pay off the mortgage on the farm.

"Just as well, with Sheriff Zach still coming out to the house looking for you."

"Zach Gillespie wants a quiet, retiring woman who wears a dress and has tea parties. Do I look like that kind of woman?" Meg shook her head, her heartache was nearly healed, though she could never look at Zach again without smiling and remembering him tied up naked.

Ruby laughed. "No, but you could be if you wanted."

Meg glanced out the window. The glow of the setting sun cast a shadow, but she could still see the dress shop down the street. After she'd spoken to this no name town sheriff, she'd spent time gazing and fingering the available dresses and the patterns of the latest fashions in the little shop. Inside these pants, a woman longed to emerge and live like a lady, not the rough, bounty hunter facade of the life she lived now.

"I'll never change for any man. As soon as we pay off the farm, then I'm going to begin my life and do things the way I want to," Meg vowed. She had dreams, she had plans, and soon, it would be her time.

Beneath her men's clothes was a woman waiting to burst out of the confines of these pants and shirt, but circumstances required she dress like a man. But the girly-girl had a hidden vice. Her own little secret pleasure…a rouge pot. Just a tiny bit of color to her lips helped her remember she was a girl. A girl who had all the same desires as every other woman.

As the sun continued its descent, cloaking the street in darkness, she knew it would soon be time to carry out their plan.

"Your weapon's ready?" Meg asked one last time. She worried about Ruby and hated leaving her alone with any outlaw for any period.

"Yes," Ruby said. "And you'll be in there with me?"

"Until you give me the signal."

"Remind me how much this guy's worth?"

"Five hundred dollars." This could be their last bounty find if things worked out like Meg planned.

Ruby smiled and walked over to the window. "Papa would be so proud of us."

Meg shook her head, knowing their Papa would have been furious at the chances they were taking. "Maybe secretly, but he'd tell us we should have taken jobs in town. He'd have been more concerned about our safety than how we were paying off the farm."

Ruby turned, her mouth twisted with displeasure. "I will never become a maid again. Never. This last year has been exciting, and criminals are too stupid to realize a pretty woman is going to pull a gun on them."

Meg nodded. In the last year, Ruby had changed and matured. She'd gone from a love-crazed girl to being driven to catch as many low-life criminals as they could. She enjoyed the chase, the thrill. "Annabelle said we need four hundred dollars more, and the farm will be mortgage free."

"Old man Clark will fall out of his chair when you pay off the note."

She smiled. "Annabelle said he wasn't too friendly when she took in the payment on the note this year. He had plans on repossessing the farm. Too bad."

"I miss Annabelle," Ruby said with a wistful whine in her voice.

"Yeah, me too. But someone had to take care of the farm, and she's good at the bookkeeping."

Meg glanced out the hotel room window and watched as men entered the saloon across the street, the doors swinging wide. Now was when her nerves had her stomach rolling, her heart racing, and fear choking her throat. What if something happened to Ruby? How could she live with herself?

"The drinking has begun," Meg said quietly, listening to the music spilling out into the street.

"And will soon end for Simon Trudeau," Ruby said laughing, her eyes shining with excitement. There was no fear in her eyes, only excited anticipation, only reckless adventure.

"The horses are saddled and ready to go. Give me your satchel and I'll secure it on your horse. I can't go in with you, or they'll make the connection between us." Meg stared at her youngest sister, fear sitting like a pit in the bottom of her stomach. "You're all set? Your weapons are ready?"

Ruby shrugged. "My knife is in my boot. My gun is in my holster." She smiled. "And my charm is ready to ensnare this poor bastard."

Meg was always stunned at how much Ruby enjoyed the chase. They used her as the bait. Then Meg would pull a gun on some poor unlucky bastard, and Ruby would tie him up. Every time before a catch, Ruby's blue eyes would sparkle and shine with excitement. She loved being a bounty hunter. She loved catching criminals, and most of all she loved playing her many roles.

They'd done everything from the distraught woman, pregnant wife, and now a saloon girl. Wherever the criminal resided, they'd lay a trap and ensnare the bastard.

"Where's your hat?" Ruby asked.

"Right here," Meg said and picked up her black cowboy hat and pulled it down tight.

But for Meg it was just a job. A means to an end. A way to earn a decent living and pay for the farm. Once they had enough money, she would retire and never chase another criminal if she could. But Ruby loved the chase, the entrapment, and the thrill of turning in the longrider.

Music echoed down the street, and Meg knew it was time. "Are you ready?"

Ruby smiled, her lips painted red, her cheeks tinted with the same color. "Let's get this done, so we can go home for a while."

"Let's go."

The two walked out of the hotel room together, but once they reached the street, Ruby walked to the saloon alone.

Meg gave her just enough time to get inside and then she followed. Time to go to work.

End of Preview
Deadly
Coming in July

Author Bio

Sylvia McDaniel

Sylvia McDaniel is a best-selling, award-winning author of western historical romance and contemporary romance novels. Known for her sweet, funny, family-oriented romances, Sylvia is the author of The Burnett Brides a western historical western series, The Cuvier Widows, a Louisiana historical series, and several short contemporary romances.

Former President of the Dallas Area Romance Authors, a member of the Romance Writers of America®, and a member of Novelists Inc, her novel, A Hero's Heart was a 1996 Golden Heart Finalist. Several other books have placed or won in the San Antonio

Romance Authors Contest, LERA Contest, Golden Network Finalist and a Carolyn Readers Finalist.

Married for nearly twenty years to her best friend, they have one dachshund that reigns as Queen Supreme Dog and a good-looking, grown son who thinks there's no place like home. Sylvia loves gardening, shopping, knitting and football (Cowboys and Bronco's fan), but not necessarily in that order.

Currently she's written eighteen novels and is hard at work on number nineteen. Be sure to sign up for her newsletter to learn about new releases, contests and every month a new subscriber is entered into a drawing for a free book.

You can write to Sylvia at P.O. Box 2542, Coppell, TX 75019 or visit her website.

Other Books by Sylvia
The Burnett Brides
The Rancher Takes a Bride
The Outlaw Takes a Bride
The Marshal Takes a Bride
The Burnett Brides Boxed Set (1-3)
The Christmas Bride

The Cuvier Women
Wronged
Betrayed
Beguiled
The Cuvier Women Boxed Set

Lipstick and Lead
Desperate
Deadly – July 2014
Dangerous – August 2014
Daring – November 2014

Not in a Series
A Hero's Heart
A Scarlet Bride

Contemporary Novels by Sylvia
My Sister's Boyfriend
The Wanted Bride
The Reluctant Santa
Kisses, Laughter & Love (Boxed Set)
Return to Cupid Texas

Made in the USA
San Bernardino, CA
08 May 2018